The Moon over the Mountain
and Other Stories

By Atsushi Nakajima

Translated by Paul McCarthy and Nobuko Ochner

This is an Autumn Hill Books Book.
Published by Autumn Hill Books, Inc.
1138 E. Benson Court
Bloomington, Indiana, 47401, USA

Original titles: "Sangetsuki" ("The Moon Over the Mountain"), first published in
1942 in the literary magazine *Bungakukai*; "Gojo shusse" ("The Rebirth of Wujing"),
"Gojo tan'i" ("On Admiration: Notes by the Monk Wujing"), "Eikyo" ("Waxing
and Waning"), and "Gyujin" ("The Bull Man"), first published in 1942 by Konnichi
no Mondaisha; "Meijinden" ("The Master"), first published in 1942 in the literary
magazine *Bunko*; "Deshi" ("The Disciple"), first published in 1943 by Chuo Koronsha;
"Riryo" ("Li Ling"), first published in 1943 in the literary magazine *Bungakukai*;
"Yofunroku" ("Forebodings"), first published in the 1959 edition of the complete works
of Nakajima Atsushi published by Bunjido Shoten.

This book has been selected by the Japanese Literature Publishing Project (JLPP), an
initiative of the Agency for Cultural Affairs of Japan.

Cover design and layout by Shawna Richter.
Cover art by Koho Yamamoto and Masa Niiya.

Autumn Hill Books ISBN-13: 978-0-982746608
Library of Congress Control Number: 2010927298

http://www.autumnhillbooks.org

Contents

The Moon over the Mountain

L i Zheng of Longxi was a very talented and learned young man who, in the last year of the Tianbao era (755), passed the qualifying examination to become a government official. He was put in charge of constabulary and military affairs in the area south of the lower reaches of the Yangzi River. But, strong-willed and self-confident, Li Zheng could not rest content with his status as a low-ranking official. He soon resigned his office, retiring to his native Guolue, where he cut off all contact with anyone outside the family and devoted his life to writing poetry. He preferred to leave a name as a poet that might last a hundred years after his death to serving as a minor official who had continually to bend the knee before vulgar superiors. But literary fame, he found, was not so easy to gain, and day by day his personal situation became more precarious. Gradually, he grew irritable. His face took on a harsh cruelty, and his body grew emaciated. His eyes had a strange glitter. There was no trace of the handsome, rosy-cheeked youth who had passed the rigorous official examination.

After a few years, unable to bear his poverty, Li Zheng bent his principles in order to provide food and clothing for his wife and children, and set off again for the east, where he accepted employment as a local official. He did this in part, too, because he had all but despaired of succeeding as a poet. By this time, his former classmates had long since climbed to high positions, and Li Zheng's self-esteem was severely wounded by having to take orders from men he had deemed dull when he himself had been so promising. A melancholy overtook him, and he grew increasingly unable to suppress a half-mad egotism.

After a year under these circumstances, Li Zheng set out on official business and, having taken lodging on the banks of a river, he at last went mad. Late one night he rose from his bed with an uncanny look on his face and rushed out of the inn, shouting unintelligible gibberish as he plunged into the darkness. He never returned, nor did searches of the nearby mountains and moors offer any clue to his whereabouts. No one knew what had become of Li Zheng.

The following year the imperial inspector Yuan Can of Chenjun received an imperial command to travel to Lingnan. Along the way, he stopped at Shangyu. Before dawn the next day, as he was preparing to set out, the man in charge of the official lodgings warned him about a man-eating tiger on the road ahead. One could proceed with safety only in broad daylight. Since it was still so early, it would be preferable to wait until the break of day, he said. Yuan Can, however, trusting in the size of his retinue, ignored this advice and set out.

By what little remained of the moonlight, they made their way through a grassy area of a forest, when suddenly out from a thicket leapt a tiger. The tiger appeared ready to attack Yuan Can when it abruptly turned around and retreated. A human voice could now be heard from the thicket, muttering over and over, "That was a very near thing."

It was a voice that Yuan Can had heard before. In the midst of his shock and fear, he remembered whose voice it was. "Why, it's my old friend, Master Li Zheng!" he cried out. Yuan Can had passed the official examinations in the same year as Li Zheng, and had been one of his very few close friends, perhaps because Yuan Can's warm and amiable personality had never clashed with Li Zheng's more extreme nature. At first there was no response from the thicket—just occasional faint sounds, as of someone weeping. After a time, a low voice replied, "Indeed, I am Li Zheng of Longxi."

Yuan Can forgot all fear and, dismounting from his horse, approached the thicket, wishing to greet his old friend whom he had not met for so many years. But why would Li Zheng not emerge and show himself? he asked. Li Zheng's voice answered that he was no longer in human form. How could he shamelessly expose himself in his degradation to his old friend? For if he did, his friend would surely feel nothing but fear and loathing. Still, having encountered Yuan Can by chance like this, he could almost forget his shame, in the joy of seeing him. "Could you somehow overlook my hideous state and talk with me for a while as your former friend Li Zheng?"

Although it seemed odd when he later recalled this moment, Yuan Can was able to accept the fact of this supernatural wonder very calmly, without doubt. He ordered his subordinate to stop the mounted party, and he stood by the thicket, conversing with the voice of the person unseen. The gossip of the capital, news of old acquaintances, Yuan Can's current position, and Li Zheng's words of congratulation on it—after speaking of all these things in the familiar manner of men who have known each other from their youth, Yuan Can asked Li Zheng how he had come to his present state. This is what the voice said:

"I was traveling about a year ago when I stopped for the night at an inn on the banks of the Ru River. I slept for a while, then suddenly awakened to hear my name being called. I went outdoors into the darkness, the voice repeatedly calling to me. I found myself running in pursuit of the voice. Furiously I ran and ran; the road entered a mountain wood, and before long, I found myself grasping at the earth with both hands as I ran. I felt an unaccountable sense of power filling my body as I leapt lightly over rocks. I noticed that fur was beginning to sprout on my hands and elbows. After daybreak, I looked into a stream to see my reflection and discovered that I had become a tiger! At first I could not believe my eyes. Then I thought it must be a dream. After all, I had had experience of dreams in which, while dreaming, I knew that it was a dream. When at last I had to acknowledge that this was no dream, I was stunned. And then afraid.

"So, then, the very strangest things can happen, I thought, and was deeply afraid. But why had this happened? I had no idea. We understand nothing, it seems. Things are pressed upon us, and we must patiently accept them, without understanding; we must go on living, without knowing why. It is our fate as creatures. At once I thought of death. But at that moment, a rabbit ran before me, and in an instant the human within me disappeared. When it reappeared, I awoke to find my mouth smeared with blood and rabbit fur scattered around me.

"That was my first experience as a tiger. And as for what I have continued to do from then until the present, I cannot bear to say. Yet for a few hours each day, my human consciousness returns; and then, as in former days, I can use human speech and think complex thoughts, and even recite passages from the Confucian classics. When, with my human consciousness, I see the results of my savagery as a tiger and reflect upon my fate, I feel misery, fear, and anger. But with time those few hours of human consciousness are growing fewer and fewer. For a while, I often wondered why I had turned into a tiger; but the other day, I found myself wondering why I had once been a human being. What a terrible thing that is! Soon, the human consciousness that I still have will vanish, buried beneath the ways of a beast—like the foundations of an ancient palace gradually being buried beneath the sands. When that happens, I will lose my past entirely and wander about as a raging tiger; and if I should happen to encounter you along the way, I would not recognize you as an old friend, but tear you to pieces, and devour you without a moment's regret."

"Actually, all beasts and men were originally something else, I am sure. At first they remember what they were; then gradually they forget, convinced that their present shape was not ever any different. But never mind about that. If the human consciousness within me were to completely disappear, I would probably be happier than I now am. Yet the human being within fears that more than anything else. How very frightening, sad, and painful that outcome seems—that I should lose all memory of having been human! How can others understand what I feel? They cannot—unless they have experienced the very same thing. But wait—I have a favor to ask of you before I cease entirely to be human."

Yuan Can and his party listened with bated breath to the extraordinary things the voice from the thicket was saying. It went on: "My sole aim in life was to win fame as a poet. But my goal has gone unachieved, and I have come to this. The several hundred poems that I wrote are unknown to the world. I doubt that anyone could even find the paper they were written on. But there are many poems that I can recite from memory, and I beg of you, please write them down and make them known. It is not that I would fancy myself a proper poet if you were to do so. No, whether the poems are good or bad, I would not rest easy in my grave without passing these poems on to later generations, since they represent my deepest passion in life, even to the point of losing my fortune and my sanity."

Yuan Can ordered one of his subordinates to take up a brush and write down what the voice from the thicket recited. Li Zheng's voice rang out clearly. He recited thirty long and short poems, elegant in expression and lofty in sentiment, all demonstrating, even upon first hearing, the poet's uncommon ability. Yet Yuan Can, although deeply impressed, could not overcome a vague unease: There could be no question that the poet's talents were first-rate, but there was a subtle lack that kept the poems from achieving the highest quality.

Li Zheng, having finished his recitation of his old poems, suddenly turned to mocking himself. "It is shameful to admit, but even now that I have sunk to such a degraded state, I still sometimes dream that a volume of my poems rests on the reading desks of the cultivated gentlemen of Chang'an. That is what I dream as I lie in my mountain cave! Is that not ridiculous—the spectacle of a man who failed to become a poet and became a tiger instead?"

Yuan Can recalled the youthful Li Zheng's penchant for self-mockery, and listened with a heavy heart. "Well," continued Li Zheng, "shall I add to the fun by composing an extemporaneous poem expressing my present feelings? Just to prove that the old Li Zheng is still alive somewhere inside this tiger. May I?"

Yuan Can again ordered his subordinate to take down the poem, which went as follows:

> Having chanced to go mad, I became a wild beast.
> Calamity piled upon calamity—I cannot escape my fate.

Who could now withstand my fangs and claws?
Yet in student days I shared your bright promise—
Now I have become a beast crouching in a thicket,
While you ride grandly in an official's carriage.
Tonight I gaze at the bright moon over the mountain.
Unable to sing an ode, I can only howl.

By then the light of the moon had grown faint, and white dew covered the ground. The chill wind that blew among the trees told the party that dawn was near. Everyone present, forgetting the strangeness of the tale, joined in respectfully lamenting this poet's misfortunes.

Li Zheng's voice went on: "I said a moment ago that I did not know why I met this fate, but when I think carefully about it, I have in fact some idea why. When I was a man, I did my best to avoid contact with others. People thought me arrogant and self-important. They did not realize it was, rather, shyness that made me act that way. Of course I was not without pride in my old reputation as a prodigy among the boys of my hometown. But it was a timid kind of pride. I hoped to make a name for myself as a poet, but I never attached myself to a teacher or sought out the company of other poets who might have helped me to improve my skill. At the same time, I had no intention of ranking myself together with the common, unpoetic herd. But this was the result of my timid pride and a disdainful shyness. Fearing that I might not be a jewel, I made no effort to polish myself; but half-believing that I might be a jewel, I could not rest content among the common clay.

"Little by little I grew apart from the world and distant from others. I fed my cowardly self-respect with dollops of rage, shame, and self-pity. We are all of us trainers of wild beasts, it is said, and the beasts in question are our own inner selves. In my case, the beast inside was my self-important sense of shame. That was my tiger, and it damaged me, brought sorrow to my wife and children, wounded my friends, and, in the end, changed my outward form into this animal that befits my inward state. I realize now that I wasted what little real talent I had. With my lips I repeated the old saw that life is far too long to do nothing, but far too short to do something of value; yet all there was in me was a cowardly fear that my lack of talent might be revealed and a lazy hatred for taking the pains needed to nurture it. There are very many men with talent far weaker than mine who have become splendid poets because they devoted themselves to polishing and improving what they had.

"Now that I have turned into a tiger, I realize that at last, and it fills me with burning regret. I can no longer live as a human being. Even if I could compose in my mind the most wonderful poem, how could it ever now be published? And my mind itself is becoming more like a tiger's with each passing day! What shall I do with my wasted past? When the pain is too great to bear, I climb up to the crag at the top of the mountain and howl into the empty valleys. I want my burning sorrow to be known. Last night I howled at the moon from that same spot, hoping that someone might somehow understand. But the animals, when they hear my voice, crouch on the ground in fear. And the mountains, trees, moon, and dew know only that a tiger has gone mad and is roaring in his rage. I could leap up to the heavens or throw myself to the ground, lamenting, yet there is none who understands what I feel—just as there was none who understood my vulnerable heart when I was a human being. If my fur looks wet, it is not only with the night dew...."

At last the surrounding darkness began to fade. From beyond the trees came the mournful sound of a horn announcing the dawn.

"And now we must say farewell, since the time of my madness, the time when I must return to my tiger state, is near," said Li Zheng's voice. "But I have yet another favor to beg before we part. It concerns my wife and children, still in Guolue. Of course, they know nothing of my fate. After you return from the south, would you tell them that I have died? I do not want them to know anything of what has passed between us today. And, although it is presumptuous of me, I beg you, have pity on their abandoned state and do what you can so they do not die of cold and hunger by some roadside. It would be a debt of gratitude I can never hope to repay."

Li Zheng having spoken these words, a loud cry came from within the thicket. Yuan Can was in tears as he assured his old friend that he would do what was asked. But Li Zheng's voice resumed a tone of self-mockery: "Were I human in the least, I would have begged this favor before anything else. A man who is more concerned about his wretched poetry than about his wife and children deserves the fate of becoming a beast!" Li Zheng then warned Yuan Can that when he made the return journey from Lingnan, he must take care not to come this way. By then, Li Zheng's madness would have returned and, unable to recognize his old friend, he might well attack him.

Finally, Li Zheng asked Yuan Can that, when he reached the top of the hill a hundred paces ahead, he look back in this direction. Li Zheng wished to show him his present form once more. It was not to impress Yuan Can with his power, but rather, by showing him the hideous beast he had become, to ensure that Yuan Can would have no desire to pass this way in order to meet him again.

Yuan Can turned toward the thicket and said heartfelt words of farewell, then mounted his horse. Once again the sound of a human voice weeping uncontrollably was heard. Yuan Can, too, wept as he rode away, glancing back several times.

When the group of travelers reached the top of the hill, they turned to look back at the grassy place in the grove. They saw a tiger spring out from the thick grass and on to the road. The tiger gazed up at the moon, already pale, having lost its brilliance, and roared mightily two times, three times, then leapt back into the brush. They never saw the tiger again.

Translated by Paul McCarthy

The Master

A man by the name of Ji Chang, who lived in Hantan, the capital of the state of Zhao, had his heart set on becoming the greatest archer in the world. Seeking a teacher, he reasoned that there was none better than Fei Wei, for Fei Wei was renowned for his ability to hit a willow leaf from a distance of a hundred paces, a hundred times out of a hundred. So Ji Chang traveled a great distance to meet Fei Wei and became his disciple.

Fei Wei's first command to his new disciple was that he learn not to blink. So Ji Chang returned home, crawled under his wife's loom, and lay flat on his back. He was trying to gaze steadily, without blinking, at the rapidly moving treadle that came close to brushing against his eyes with each downward motion. His wife, who did not understand the reason for this, was shocked. As she sat in her unusual position at the loom, she did not wish to have her husband staring up at her from his unusual one on the floor. Ji Chang scolded her and demanded she keep weaving. Day after day he practiced not blinking in this posture. After two years, Ji Chang no longer blinked even if the under-treadle grazed his eyelashes each time it rushed by. Finally one day he crawled out from under the loom. He had reached the point of not blinking even if the sharp tip of an awl grazed his eyelids. Even if sparks shot into his eyes or a cloud of dust rose up, he did not blink. His eyelids had forgotten how to signal the muscles that should have closed them, and even at night when he was fast asleep, his eyes remained wide open. At last, when a tiny spider began to spin its web in the spaces among his eyelashes, Ji Chang felt he had learned enough to report back to his master Fei Wei.

Fei Wei listened to his disciple and remarked: "Not blinking is not by itself sufficient for receiving my teaching. Now you must learn to see. When you have learned to see, and the small seems large, and the faint seems clear, come back to me."

Ji Chang returned home again. In the seam of his undergarment he found a louse that had taken up residence. He tied it to a strand of his hair, which he hung in a south-facing window. He spent the whole day staring at the louse, and this he did, day after day after day. At first the louse was, of course, just a louse. After two or three days, it was still a louse. But after ten days, the louse seemed (was this his imagination?) to be a bit bigger. By the end of the third month, the insect was the size of a silkworm. The scenery outside the window where the louse was hanging changed as well. The springtime sun, which had shone so pleasantly, quickly turned into the blazing sun of summer; and no sooner had the migrating geese flown through clear autumn skies than sleet began to fall from cold, gray winter ones. Ji Chang patiently gazed at the tiny blood-sucking, itch-inducing arthropod that dangled from the end of his strand of hair. Three years passed, the first louse having been replaced by tens upon tens of its fellows. One day Ji Chang realized that the louse in the window had grown to the size of a horse. "This is it!" he cried, slapping his knee. Stepping outdoors, he could hardly believe his eyes: People were as tall as towers, and horses were as big as mountains! Pigs seemed like hills, chickens like castle lookout-posts. Dancing for joy, Ji Chang went into his house, focused on the louse hanging in the window, and set a mugwort arrow to his bow made of horn. When the arrow was shot, it went straight through the heart of the insect, without severing the hair to which the louse was tied.

Ji Chang went immediately to Fei Wei and announced his feat.

His teacher leaped up and, striking himself on the chest, praised his disciple for the first time: "Well done, well done!" Then without reservation, he proceeded to teach Ji Chang the secrets and mysteries of the art of archery.

Ji Chang's five years spent training his eyes proved effective, and from this point his learning progressed rapidly indeed. Ten days after the master had begun to share the secrets of the art with him, his student was able to shoot his arrows at willow leaves from a hundred paces and hit his target every time. When, after twenty days, he drew a sturdy bow with a full bowl of water balanced on his right elbow, not only was his aim perfect but the water in the bowl did not move. When, after one month, he attempted shooting one hundred arrows in quick succession, the first arrow hit the target, the second arrow did not fail to hit and penetrate the notch of the first, and the point of the third arrow sank deeply into the notch of the second. Arrow after arrow flew to its mark, and since the later arrows always lodged themselves in the notch of the previous arrow, not one fell to the ground. In the twinkling of an eye, the one hundred arrows had formed a single unbroken line from the target, with the notch of the last arrow seemingly still fitted to the bowstring. "Splendid!" shouted Fei Wei, who was watching from the sidelines.

After two months, Ji Chang returned home where, quarreling with his wife over a trivial matter, he decided he would teach her a lesson. He fitted an arrow that had been made in Qiwei to his finest bow, pulled it taut, and let fire at his wife's eye. The arrow took off three of her eyelashes as it sped by, but his wife didn't notice a thing—she just kept scolding away, without so much as a blink. The speed of his arrows and precision of his aim had reached such a level as that.

Ji Chang now had nothing more to learn from his master, and one day a wicked thought entered his mind: In the art of archery Ji Chang's only rival was Fei Wei himself. In order to become the very best archer in the world, Ji Chang would have to eliminate his teacher. He quietly waited for his opportunity. One day he encountered Fei Wei walking alone in the fields outside the town. Deciding at once to act, Ji Chang fitted an arrow to his bow and took aim. Sensing the attack, Fei Wei took his bow and made ready. Master and disciple sent arrows flying at one another, but each time the arrows collided in midair and fell to the ground. The fallen arrows did not raise even a puff of dust, so perfect were the skills of the two men. Finally, Fei Wei exhausted his supply of arrows, while Ji Chang had one arrow left. "This is my chance!" the disciple thought, and shot his arrow. In an instant, Fei Wei broke off a twig from a wild rose bush and, using the tip of a thorn, deflected the point of Ji Chang's last arrow. Realizing that his wicked ambition could not be fulfilled, Ji Chang felt ethical remorse of a sort that would never have arisen had he managed to succeed. Fei Wei, for his part, relieved at having escaped the crisis and gratified at the excellence of his skill, quite forgot any ill-will he might have felt against his foe. The two men ran toward each other and, meeting in the middle of the field, embraced, tears expressive of the beautiful love of master and disciple flowing, for a time. (It would be wrong to view this from the standpoint of present-day morality. When Duke Huan of Qi, a noted gourmet, demanded a rare dish that he had never yet tasted, his chef Yi Ya steamed his own son and offered the flesh to the duke. And on the night of his father's death, the sixteen-year-old first emperor of Qin sexually used his father's favorite concubine three times. That was the kind of age it was.)

Even as the two men tearfully embraced, Fei Wei was thinking how dangerous it would be if his disciple should make another such attempt and decided to distract Ji Chang by giving him a new set of goals. So he said to his dangerous disciple: "I have taught you everything I know. If you wish to penetrate the further mysteries of this art, go west and, crossing Mount Da Xing, climb to the top of Mount Huo. There you will find Master Gan Ying, the greatest practitioner of archery of this or any age. Compared to his art, our skills are mere child's play. From now on, there can be no teacher for you apart from Gan Ying."

Ji Chang set out immediately for the west. Fei Wei's words about their skills being like child's play had wounded his pride. If that were true, he was still far from his goal of becoming the greatest archer in the world. He hurried along the road, eager to test his skills against this master to see if they were, in fact, "like child's play." The soles of his feet grew blistered and his legs scraped as he climbed the precipitous crags and crossed narrow plank-bridges until, after a month, he at last reached the mountaintop.

Ji Chang had roused himself to a pitch of rivalry, but it was a doddering old man with mild, sheep-like eyes whom he encountered. Gan Ying must have been over one hundred years old. His white beard dragged along the ground as he walked, stooped over with age.

Thinking the old man might be deaf, Ji Chang in a loud voice hurriedly announced his purpose in coming. He wanted the master to judge his skills, he said. Not waiting for a reply, he pulled out a special arrow and with his large bow made of willow wood wound with hemp, took aim at a flock of migratory birds flying high above them. At once, five geese plummeted from the clear blue sky.

"Quite well done," said the old man, with a gentle smile. "But that is what we call 'shooting by shooting.' You seem not yet to know about 'shooting by not shooting,' young man."

The old hermit led a rather petulant Ji Chang to the top of a steep cliff about two hundred paces away. Beneath them was a sheer drop of hundreds of feet, like a gigantic screen; just a glimpse of the stream that was visible as a fine thread far below was enough to make one feel dizzy. The old man ran on to a rock perilously perched half over the edge and, turning to Ji Chang, said, "How about showing me that trick of yours out here?" The younger man could hardly back out now. But when Ji Chang stepped out on to the rock, he felt it shift a bit. He plucked up his courage and was about to fit an arrow to his bowstring when a pebble fell from the cliff side, which he watched as it plunged downward. Ji Chang found himself flattened prostrate against the rock, sweating even to the heels of his feet, his legs trembling. The old man laughed as he extended a hand to help Ji Chang down from the rock. He then got back on to the rock himself and said, "Well, then, perhaps I should show you how to shoot?" Ji Chang's heart was pounding and his face was deathly pale, but still he noticed something very odd: "What about the bow? The bow . . . ?" The old hermit's hands were empty. "The bow, you say?" he said, laughing. "So long as a bow and arrow are needed, we just have 'shooting by shooting.' For 'shooting by not shooting' there is no need for a black-lacquered bow or sharp stone-tipped arrows."

High, high above them in the sky, a single hawk was slowly circling. Gan Ying gazed for a while at the bird that seemed as small as a sesame seed, then fitted an invisible arrow to his formless bow, drew it back so strongly that the bow became as round as the full moon, and shot. The hawk plummeted through the air like a stone, without so much as a flap of its wings.

Ji Chang was terrified: He had caught a first glimpse of the most profound depths of the art of archery.

Ji Chang stayed with the old master for nine years, but what training he engaged in during that time no one knows.

When he finally came down from the mountain, people were amazed at the change in him. That proud, indomitable look was gone, replaced by an expressionless face, like that of a fool or a wooden doll. When he paid a visit to Fei Wei, however, his old teacher cried out in admiration: "Now indeed you have become a great master! Someone like myself cannot compare with you at all."

The city of Hantan, welcoming Ji Chang back as the greatest archer in the world, was abuzz with expectation of the wondrous skills he would surely put on display. But Ji Chang seemed to have no interest at all in doing so. In fact, he never took his bow in hand; it seemed that he had thrown away the willow-wood bow wound with hemp that he had carried with him into the mountains. When someone asked him the reason, Ji Chang answered listlessly: "Perfect action lies in inaction, perfect speech abandons words, and perfect archery means never shooting." The perspicacious citizens of the capital understood at once, and took especial pride in their master archer who never touched a bow. The less Ji Chang had to do with archery, the greater grew his reputation as a matchless master archer.

Rumors of various sorts spread among the populace: Every night in the hours just after midnight, people heard a bow twanging from Ji Chang's roof, yet there was no one to be seen. It was said to be the god of archery who dwelt within the master archer, leaving his body while he slept in order to guard him from evil spirits in the night. A merchant who lived nearby claimed to have seen with his own eyes Ji Chang mounted on a cloud above his house, taking his bow in hand for once, and vying with Yi and Yang Youji, master archers of a previous age. The arrows shot by the three vanished, he said, between the regions of Orion and Sirius, leaving pale blue trails of light in the night sky. Then there was the burglar who confessed that he had tried to sneak into Ji Chang's house: When he placed a foot on the outer wall, a blast of air burst from inside the silent house, struck him on the forehead, and knocked him off the wall. From then on, ill-intentioned persons took care to give his residence a wide berth, and the cleverer birds of passage no longer flew over his house.

As his fame rose to the very heavens, Master Ji Chang was growing old. His mind, which had long since lost interest in the shooting of arrows, became more pure, tranquil, and detached from things with every passing day. His wooden doll-like face lost all expression whatsoever; he rarely said a word, and it became hard to tell whether he was still breathing. "I no longer know the difference between 'me' and 'him', or the distinction between right and wrong. My eye seems like an ear, my ear like a nose, and my nose like a mouth." So spoke the old master in his last years.

Forty years after he had left the hermitage of Gan Ying, Ji Chang passed from this world quietly—truly, as quietly as smoke disappearing. During those four decades, he never spoke of archery, and still less would he have actually taken bow and arrow in hand. Now, as an author, I would like nothing better than to have the old master finish with some splendid action so as to make his status as a real master perfectly clear. Yet at the same time, I must not distort the facts recorded in the ancient documents. All we know is that he passed his last years in a state of nonaction. Nothing else is known, except the following curious story.

It happened one or two years before his death, it seems. One day Ji Chang was invited to a friend's house, and there he saw a certain object. He was sure he had seen one before, but, for the life of him, he could not recall its name or purpose. The old man asked his host, "What do you call this thing, and what do you use it for?" The friend thought his guest was joking, and just grinned foolishly. Old Ji Chang asked again, with great seriousness, but still his host smiled vaguely, unable to guess what was on his mind. Only when, for the third time, Ji Chang asked the same questions with absolute earnestness did his host's expression change to one of amazement. He looked his guest straight in the eye, and when he had determined that Ji Chang was neither joking nor mad, and that he himself had not misheard, he cried out, stuttering in confusion tinged with terror: "Oh, Master, archer without peer in any age! Can you have forgotten what a bow is? Even its very name and purpose?"

It is said that, for some time afterward, in the capital of Hantan, artists hid their brushes, musicians cut the strings of their zithers, and carpenters were ashamed to be seen with the tools of their trade in hand.

Translated by Paul McCarthy

The Bull Man

When Shusun Bao of Lu was a young man, he fled for a time to Qi to avoid political unrest. Along the way, he met a beautiful woman at Gengzong, on the northern border of Lu. They became intimate, and spent the night together; the next morning he parted from her and crossed into Qi. He settled there and married the daughter of a high official of the Guo clan, with whom he had two children. He had quite forgotten about his earlier tryst of one night by the roadside.

Then one evening he had a dream. The atmosphere was heavy and oppressive, and a premonition of misfortune filled his quiet room. Suddenly, soundlessly, the ceiling began to descend. It came down very gradually, but most certainly. With each instant the atmosphere in the room grew heavier, and his breath more labored. He struggled to move, but found himself immobilized face up on the bed. Though of course he could not see it, he knew with absolute certainty that the black sky was pressing down upon the ceiling with the weight of a huge rock. Little by little the ceiling came closer, and as an unbearable heaviness began to press upon his chest, he glanced to one side and saw a man standing there—it was a hunchback with fearfully dark skin, deep-set eyes, and a mouth that protruded like an animal's snout. His appearance was that of a jet-black bull.

"Help me, bull!" Shusun Bao found himself begging, and the black man stretched out a hand to push up against the infinite weight descending from above. With his other hand he gently stroked Shusun Bao's chest, causing the oppressive feeling to vanish. "Oh, thank heavens!" Shusun Bao said aloud, and woke up.

The next morning he assembled his retainers and servants, but there was none who resembled the bull man in his dream. For some time afterward he carefully, but unobtrusively, observed all who came and went in the Qi capital, but he never encountered anyone like the bull man.

Some years later there was another political upheaval in his native state, and Shusun Bao, leaving his family behind in Qi, immediately returned to Lu. It was only after being appointed as an official at the court of Lu that he ventured to summon his wife and children to join him. His wife, however, had by then entered into an affair with an official in Qi and made no effort to rejoin her husband in Lu. In the end only his two sons, Mengbing and Zhongren, came to live with their father.

One morning a woman bearing the gift of a pheasant came to see him. At first Shusun Bao had no idea who she was, but as they talked, he realized she was the woman with whom he had spent the night at Gengzong more than ten years before. He asked if she had come alone, and she answered that her son was with her. She went on to say that he was also the son of Shusun Bao from the night they had slept together. When the boy was brought before him, Shusun Bao cried out in amazement. He was a dark-skinned hunchback with deep-set eyes, exactly resembling the black bull man who had saved Shusun Bao in his dream. Shusun Bao muttered the word "bull" to himself, and the boy responded with a look of surprise. Even more surprised at that, Shusun Bao asked him his name, and the lad said, "I am called Bull, sir."

Both mother and son were immediately taken into the household, the boy becoming one of the pages; and from then on, even after he became an adult, this bull-like son of Shusun Bao was known as "Bull the Page." Despite his appearance, he was quite clever and proved a very useful servant, but there was always something melancholy about him, and he did not join in the pleasures and amusements of his fellow pages. He never smiled at anyone apart from his master, who was in turn very fond of him and eventually entrusted him with the management of the entire household.

That dark face with its deep-set eyes and protuberant mouth had a funny charm of its own on the rare occasions that it was lit up by a smile. One got the impression that someone with such a comical face would be incapable of any wicked plots. This was the face he showed to those above him. When he was lost in thought with a sullen look on his face, on the other hand, there was something inhuman and strangely cruel about him. And it was this face that his fellow servants found so frightening. Bull seemed capable of using these two different faces without even trying.

Shusun Bao had limitless trust in Bull, but he had no intention of making him his heir. As private secretary-*cum*-butler, he was peerless; but he hardly seemed suited in terms of appearance to become the head of one of the great families of Lu. Bull of course understood this, and was always extremely courteous toward Shusun Bao's other sons, particularly the brothers Mengbing and Zhongren. They, for their part, found him a little weird, and more than a little contemptible. That they did not feel much jealousy despite their father's affection for Bull was due to their confidence in their own superiority.

Beginning around the time Duke Xiang of Lu died and was succeeded by the young Duke Zhao, Shusun Bao's health began to fail. He had gone to Qiuyou to hunt, and on the way back he caught a bad chill and had to take to his bed after arriving home, becoming gradually unable to stand. Everything, from seeing to Shusun Bao's personal needs to relaying orders from his sickbed, was left in the hands of Bull the Page. Yet Bull's attitude toward Mengbing and his brother became all the more humble.

Before he took to his bed, Shusun Bao had decided to have a bell cast on behalf of Mengbing, his eldest son. As he said at the time, "You are not yet on close terms with the various officials of this country. When the bell is done, you should give a banquet and invite all the high officials of Lu." Now it was obvious from this remark that Shusun Bao had decided on Mengbing as his heir.

As he lay ill, the casting of the bell was completed. Mengbing, making plans for the banquet, asked Bull to consult his father as to the right day for the banquet since, except in case of emergency, no one other than Bull was allowed into the sickroom. Bull agreed to the request and went into the sickroom, but he said nothing at all about the matter to Shusun Bao. He came back out to Mengbing and, setting an arbitrary date, represented this as the will of the master. When the appointed day came, Mengbing welcomed his guests to a lavish banquet and tolled the new bell for the first time. Shusun Bao heard the sound from his sickbed and, wondering about it, asked Bull what it meant. Bull replied that a banquet was being held at Mengbing's residence to celebrate the new bell, with many guests in attendance. The invalid's face turned red as he cried out, "How dare he take it upon himself to act like my heir without so much as asking my permission!" Bull the Page did not fail to add that several guests related to the youth's mother had come all the way from Qi to celebrate. He knew very well that any mention of Shusun Bao's former wife, who had betrayed him, always infuriated the master. The invalid tried to get up, but Bull held him back, saying that the master must not exert himself.

"He's decided I'm as good as dead and he can do whatever the hell he pleases!" Shusun Bao now cried, gnashing his teeth. "Never mind. Throw him in prison," he ordered. "And if he resists, kill him!"

The banquet ended, and the young heir of the Shusun house bade a courteous farewell to his many guests; by the next morning, his corpse was lying where it had been tossed, in a thicket behind his house.

Mengbing's younger brother Zhongren was on good terms with a certain attendant of Duke Zhao, and one day when he was visiting the palace to see his friend, he happened to catch the duke's attention. Zhongren said a few words in response to an inquiry of the duke and made a very good impression, leading the duke personally to give him a jade waist-pendant as he left the Court.

Now Zhongren was a gentle youth, and not wanting to wear such an object without first informing his father of the honor he'd received, he asked Bull to pass on the story and show the pendant to his invalid father. Bull took the object and went into the sickroom, but he did not show it to Shusun Bao, nor did he mention the presence of Zhongren. He came back out to Zhongren and said, "Your father is very pleased and wants you to begin wearing the pendant at once." Zhongren did as instructed.

Some days later, Bull made a suggestion to Shusun Bao: Since Mengbing was now dead and Zhongren would become the heir, why not arrange for a formal audience with Duke Zhao? "No," replied Shusun Bao, "I have not made a decision yet, so it is too early for that." "Whatever your thoughts may be about the matter, it appears your son has decided in his own mind that he is to be the heir and has in fact already had a kind of audience with the duke," Bull responded. "Nonsense! How could that be?" said the invalid. Bull assured him that Zhongren had recently been wearing a jade pendant given him by the duke. The youth was summoned, and indeed he was wearing a jade pendant, which he admitted was a gift from the duke. His father raised his weakened body from the bed in anger. Zhongren was not permitted to say a word by way of explanation, and was told to get out of his father's sight and not leave his own quarters.

That night Zhongren fled in secret to Qi.

As Shusun Bao's illness grew worse, it became urgent that he think about who was to be his heir. At this point, Shusun Bao decided to call Zhongren back, and told Bull to send a message to him. Bull left the sickroom as if to carry out the order, but of course he sent no message to Zhongren in Qi. Instead, he reported to Shusun Bao that his son's reply was that he had no intention of returning to so inhuman a father.

Now, at last, doubts about this retainer of his began to arise in the master's mind. And so he asked sharply, "Are you telling me the truth?" "Why would I lie to you?" answered Bull, but the invalid saw that his servant's lips were curled in a mocking smile. It was the first time he had seen this since the man had come into his service. Furious, the invalid tried to rise from his bed but had not the strength and collapsed from the effort. And now that face like a black bull's was gazing down on him coldly, with a look of contempt. It was the cruel face he had shown only to his fellows and subordinates. Shusun Bao could summon his relatives and other retainers only via this man—that was the established practice now. That night, the invalid official thought of his son Mengbing, whom he had had killed, and he wept in frustration and chagrin.

The next day, the cruelties began. It had been customary for the invalid's meals to be brought to an adjoining room and carried from there to his bedside by Bull, since the sick man "did not want to have contact with others," as Bull said. Now he no longer offered the invalid any food. He himself ate everything that had been prepared for the master, and put the empty dishes out into the corridor for retrieval. The kitchen staff believed that Shusun Bao had eaten it all. When the invalid complained of hunger, the bull man sneered in silence. He no longer bothered to reply. As for Shusun Bao, there was no longer anyone he could call on for help.

It happened that Du Xie, the household chamberlain, came one day to pay his respects to the master in his illness. Shusun Bao complained bitterly about Bull the Page's treatment of him; but knowing how greatly the master had always trusted Bull, Du Xie took it all as a joke and paid no attention. And when the invalid continued to rail even more vehemently against his attendant, Du Xie wondered if he had not lost his senses due to fever. Bull, standing to one side, gave Du Xie, a glance that suggested he was at his wits' end dealing with this mentally disturbed man. Finally the invalid, shedding tears of rage, pointed with a thin, enfeebled hand at a sword and cried out to Du Xie, "Kill him with this! Quickly! Kill him!" Then, realizing he was being regarded as nothing but a madman, Shusun Bao began to wail, his wasted body atremble. Du Xie exchanged a look with Bull and then with furrowed brow quietly left the room. Now that the guest had gone, an uncanny smile began to play over the bull man's face.

Starved and exhausted, the sick man wept as he began to drift off. Did he dream in his sleep, or was it a hallucination he was seeing? A solitary lamp burned silently in the room, the air was thick and stagnant, the atmosphere menacing. The lamplight was dim and without radiance. As the sick man gazed at it, it began to seem far, far away—ten or twenty *li* distant. The ceiling began gradually to descend, just as it had in his dream of years ago, until slowly but surely the weight of it pressed upon him. He wanted to escape, but could not move even a leg. Glancing to one side, he saw a black bull man standing there. He begged for help, but this time the bull man did not extend his hand. He stood, silent and erect, with a sneer on his face. Shusun Bao made one last desperate plea, and suddenly the bull man's face took on a hard, angry look as he gazed down on the sick man, moving not so much as an eyebrow.

The jet-black weight bore down upon his chest and Shusun Bao let out a final scream—and then returned to his senses.

Night seemed to have fallen, and in a corner of the dark room a pale lamplight flickered. It was probably this that he had seen in his dream. When he glanced to one side, he saw the face of Bull the Page, exactly as he had seen it in his dream, gazing quietly down at him with a cold cruelty that was quite inhuman. It no longer seemed human at all, but rather an object rooted in a black primeval chaos. Shusun Bao felt chilled to the marrow of his bones. It was not the terror one might feel toward a killer. It was closer to the humble fear one might feel in the face of the harsh malice of the world. His anger of just a few moments before was now overwhelmed by a fatal dread. He no longer had the spirit to oppose this man in any way.

Three days later Shusun Bao, the famed official of the state of Lu, starved to death.

Translated by Paul McCarthy

Forebodings

She was a quiet, reserved woman. Her beauty was undeniable, but it was passive and doll-like, appearing at times close to stupidity. She seemed to look with amazement upon the various incidents that arose around her and on her account. Indeed, she seemed entirely unaware that they had been provoked by her. She might have been aware, and just been pretending not to be. But even if she were, no one could say whether she felt pride, or thought that the incidents were troublesome, or was mocking the foolish men involved. At any rate, there was not a trace of haughtiness in her manner.

Sometimes her face, normally as still as a man-made object, would take on an intense inner radiance. Her earlobes would flush, deepening to a ruby tint, and it was as if lamps had suddenly been lit within two small shrines of cool pure-white stone. And the jet-black pupils of her eyes would gleam entrancingly. When this occurred, the woman would be transformed into an extraordinary being, and the men who chanced to meet her at these moments would fall under her spell, forgetting themselves in folly beyond the bounds of the quotidian.

Xiaji, wife of Yushu, a high official of the land of Chen, was the daughter of Duke Mu of Zheng. In the first year of the reign of King

Ding of Zhou, her father died; and her elder brother Ziban, who had succeeded him, died by violence the following year. The liaison between Xiaji and Duke Ling of Chen had begun around that time, so it was of long duration. It was not the result of force on the part of a lecherous sovereign. Developments of this sort were, to Xiaji, as natural as water seeking its level. She knew neither excitement nor regret: these events simply happened before one quite understood how. Her husband Yushu was a typical good-natured coward. He seemed to be vaguely cognizant of what was taking place, but this mattered little. If Xiaji felt no guilt toward her husband, she also felt no contempt for him. But she did make a point of treating him more lovingly than she had before.

One day Duke Ling was making sport of the noblemen Kong Ning and Yi Xingfu, and playfully gave them a glimpse of his under-robe, which was a luxurious-looking woman's under-garment. The two noblemen were startled because, truth to tell, each of them was wearing a similar under-robe that originally belonged to Xiaji. Did Duke Ling know? The noblemen knew of each other's affair with Xiaji. But given that the duke had shown them that under-robe, did he not perhaps also know about their affairs with her? Ought they to respond to their sovereign's gesture with complicit, flattering smiles? Nervously, the men tried to read Duke Ling's expression. All they found was a complacent, lascivious smile that seemed without ulterior motive. The two courtiers felt relieved. A few days later, they were so bold as to show Duke Ling their own luxurious-looking under-garments. A gentleman named Xieye, who was fearless and straightforward, spoke forthrightly to the duke: "If the ruler and nobles reveal themselves as having acted indecently, will not the ministers and retainers follow their example? Moreover, there will be scandalous talk. Therefore, my lord, I beg you to put aside such behavior."

In this period, the land of Chen was wedged between the states of Jin and Chu; if Chen allied itself with either, it would be attacked by the other. This was not the occasion for the ruler to give himself to erotic pleasures. There was nothing the duke could do but apologize to the gentleman, promising that he would mend his ways. Kong Ning and

Yi Xingfu, hearing this, insisted that this subject who knew no fear of his lord be eliminated; Duke Ling made no effort to restrain them. The next day, Xieye was stabbed to death by an unknown assailant.

Eventually the good-natured husband Yushu also died an unaccountable death.

There was almost no jealousy between Duke Ling on the one hand and the two noblemen on the other—such was the aura cast by Xiaji upon them. One day when the three obsessed men were drinking together at Xiaji's house, her son Zhengshu happened to pass in front of them. Viewing his retreating figure, Duke Ling said to Xingfu, "Zengshu looks a lot like you!" Xingfu laughed and immediately shot back, "Not at all! It's you he looks like, my lord!" Young Zhengshu heard these remarks clearly. Questions about his father's death, anger at his mother's carryings-on, and humiliation regarding his own existence—all these at once flamed up within him.

When the banquet ended and the duke left the hall, an arrow flew toward him and lodged in his chest. From the darkness of a distant stable, the glittering eyes of Zhengshu peered out. A second arrow was already fitted to the bow by a hand that trembled with despair and rage.

Terrified, Kong Ning and Yi Xingfu immediately fled to Chu, without daring to return to their homes.

The practice of the period was that when there was a rebellion in one state, a powerful state would use the instability as an excuse to invade, under the guise of pacification. As soon as King Zhuang of Chu learned that Duke Ling of Chen had been killed, he led his army into the Chen capital. Zhengshu was captured and executed at Limen—tied to two chariots and torn apart.

Xiaji, the cause of the disturbances in Chen, was from the start the object of the curious gaze of the Chu generals. Expecting her to be a wicked femme fatale, they were disappointed to find a rather quiet, ordinary-looking woman. She seemed very composed regarding the troubles that had destroyed her country, as if she alone were innocent of any blame, like a child that cannot be held responsible for its actions. Nor did she seem upset by the fate of her only son, so cruelly executed. In the presence of the Chu king and his noblemen, passing into and out of her chambers, she kept her gaze modestly down. When King Zhuang made his triumphant return to Chu, he took Xiaji with him. His plan was to add her to the women in his palace.

Qu Wu, commonly known as Ziling, also called Wuchen, remonstrated with the king over this: "It is not right. To be greedy for erotic pleasure is to be licentious. Licentiousness is to be severely punished. In the *History of Zhou* it is said: 'One should manifest one's virtue and refrain from vice.' My lord, endeavor to follow this, I pray you!" And King Zhuang, whose political ambitions were even stronger than his lust, immediately accepted Wuchen's remonstrance.

Zifan, the chief minister of Chu, wished to wed Xiaji, but once again Wuchen intervened: "Is Xiaji not an ill-omened woman? She caused her elder brother to die young, she murdered her husband, she killed her lord, she sent her son to be slaughtered, she brought about the exile of two courtiers, and she destroyed the land of Chen. There could hardly be another woman as inauspicious as she! There are many beautiful women in the world—why choose her?" Zifan, out of a twisted sense of injured vanity, reluctantly gave up his plan to marry her. In the end, Xiaji was given to Xianglao, the official in charge of Chu's archers. She calmly accepted this. Indeed, there was no one who was as accepting of what she was given as this woman. And then, before one knew it, and without she herself being aware of it, she would corrupt the man she had been given, and drive him quite mad.

In the following year, the tenth of the reign of King Ding of Zhou, the armies of Jin and Chu clashed in the region of Bi. Chu was soundly defeated. Xianglao was killed in battle and his corpse taken by the enemy. His son Heiyao was by now a strong young man. Dressed in the robes of mourning, he and Xiaji, mindless of the death of father and husband, soon began to indulge in erotic pleasure with one another.

Wuchen, the master of oracles who had earlier remonstrated with King Zhuang and Zifan, finally made his approach to Xiaji. An experienced strategist, he did not seek to gain her favors immediately. Expending vast amounts of gold and silver, he laid a plan with her native state of Zheng, for he knew that it would be impossible for him, in his position, to wed Xiaji in the land of Chu. Thus, in time, a message was sent to Chu from Zheng, stating that Xianglao's body would be sent there from Jin, and that Xiaji should return to Zheng to receive the remains of her husband. King Zhuang was uncertain about the trustworthiness of this message and summoned Wuchen to ask his opinion.

"It seems trustworthy," was Wuchen's reply. "We have a captive from the battle at Bi. His father is a trusted minister of the lord of Jin, and the family has many connections in Zheng. I am sure Jin will request a prisoner exchange, using Zheng as intermediary. And they will offer to return our young nobleman Guchen, now their captive, as well as Xianglao's remains."

So King Zhuang agreed to Xiaji's return to her native Zheng. Xiaji, of course, was well aware of Wuchen's designs. When she left for Zheng, she mused out loud, "I will not return without my husband's remains." Not a soul who heard this took it as meaning: "There seems little chance that I will receive my husband's remains, so I doubt I will ever come back." As she stood dressed in the all-black robes of mourning that hid her charms, she was the very picture of the pious widow concerned only with retrieving her husband's body.

She parted with Heiyao very easily. Upon her arrival in Zheng, a secret messenger from Wuchen immediately informed the Zheng ruler that Wuchen wished to make her his wife. Duke Xiang of Zheng agreed to this. It did not mean, however, that Xiaji had already become Wuchen's.

King Zhuang of Chu died and was succeeded by King Gong. The latter allied himself with Qi in order to attack Lu; and in order to let Qi know when he planned to dispatch his troops, he sent Wuchen as his emissary. Wuchen gathered his belongings to depart. On the road he met one Shen Shuguei, who said to him: "Looking so aroused and happy in the midst of war among three states—how strange!" After Wuchen reached Zheng, he had his vice-emissary return to Chu with gifts, and he went off with Xiaji. She accompanied him, but without enthusiasm, as they made for Qi; but its army had just been defeated at the battle of An so they fled to Jin instead, where, through the good offices of the influential minister Xi Zhi, Wuchen was put in charge of Xing, an outlying district.

Zifan of Chu, who had been stopped from marrying Xiaji by Wuchen, who then made off with her, ground his teeth in fury. He sent elaborate bribes to Jin in an effort to keep Wuchen from becoming an official there, but all for naught. In frustration, he slaughtered Wuchen's family, including his sons Ziyan and Zidang, as well as Heiyao, Xiaji's stepson, and claimed their property. Even then, he remained dissatisfied.

Wuchen at once sent a letter from Jin, cursing Zifan and vowing vengeance. He asked the ruler of Jin to send him as an envoy to Wu so that Jin and Wu could make a concerted pincer attack against Chu. Chao and Xu, tributary states to the south of Chu, were attacked by Wu; and Zifan was exhausted from as many as seven defensive campaigns in a single year. Several years later, accepting responsibility for the defeat at Yanling, Zifan killed himself by cutting his own throat.

Xiaji seemed at last to have settled down as Wuchen's wife. She practiced self-restraint and never went against the will of Heaven. It was hard to believe that this was the bewitching creature who had once thrown the two states of Chen and Chu into disarray. Yet Wuchen did not feel at ease. He knew what sort of woman she had been. She seemed not to age at all. She must have been nearly fifty years old, yet her skin glowed like a virgin's. Her strange youthfulness was a source of endless worry to Wuchen. He trained the serving girls and boys to spy on her. Their reports only served to confirm Xiaji's chastity. Wuchen was not so good-natured as to give total credence to these reports, and neither was he so nonchalant as to stop the surveillance. He was perplexed at why he had pursued this woman with such fervor. When he recalled her affair with Xianglao's son Heiyao, he could not help having suspicions about his own adult sons It was in part from such considerations that he had left his son Huyong behind in Wu for so long.

He reflected on how few people there were in his immediate vicinity ever since the "chaste" Xiaji had come to live with him, and was amazed at his isolation. He had prided himself on beating out his competitors with strategy and thus gaining possession of what he desired, but who had really gained possession of whom? He no longer desired Xiaji. He had become a different person. But his craving to possess the woman had become an autonomous thing: It held on as a kind of habit, a compulsion, which continued to exert its control....

He had to acknowledge that his life was already rushing toward decline. He was conscious of a weakening of his mental and physical powers. Once, in the evening twilight, gazing at Xiaji's profile as she sat upright, appearing like a legendary white fox that has exercised her magical powers, he understood for the first time the high price he had paid. He was horrified; yet in the next moment, an unaccountable sense of amusement welled up within him. What a foolish dance! And the white fox Xiaji, too, was in the end merely another puppet on a string.... The meaninglessness of his whole life lay open for viewing, like someone else's affair.

He started to laugh, loudly, emptily, as if the spirit of the puppeteer who had made them dance had taken possession of him.

Translated by Paul McCarthy

The Disciple

One

There was a young, chivalrous ronin from Bian, in the land of Lu, whose proper name was Zhongyu but who was generally known as Zilu. Zilu had gotten it into his head that Kong Qiu, the scholarly gentleman from Zou who had lately been gaining a reputation for wisdom, could use some humiliation. This "wise man" was a fake, Zilu decided, and set off for Kong Qiu's house with his hair wild and bristling, his cap tilted back, and the skirt of his robe tucked up behind, as if ready for a fight. From his left hand dangled a rooster and from his right a pig, and he looked very fierce indeed. His plan was to upset the scholar as he practiced the zither, lectured, and recited poetry by shaking the rooster until it crowed and pinching the pig until it oinked.

Thus began the dialogue between the young man, who had rushed in with baleful eyes and obnoxious animal sounds, and Confucius (as Kong Qiu is known in the West), benignly seated on his chair, wearing a scholar's round hat, decorated shoes, and ornaments hanging from his waistband.

"What is it that you like?" asked Confucius.

"I like a long sword!" the young man replied boldly.

Confucius could not help smiling at his childish pride. Yet he could also see, in the young man's strong face, with its thick eyebrows, sharp, clear gaze, and ruddy complexion, a wonderful honesty.

Confucius put another question to him: "What about learning?"

"Learning! How could that be of any use?" Since this was what he had wanted to say in the first place, Zilu shouted this.

Now, when the power of learning was called into question, Confucius could not dismiss the matter with a smile. In earnest, he began to explain the value of learning: If a ruler of men lacks ministers to remonstrate with him, he will depart from what is right; and if a gentleman lacks friends to teach him, he will lose the chance to listen and learn. Are not trees made to grow straight by being bound with ropes? If horses need whips and bows need repair, how could a man not need a doctrine to correct his willful character? It is only after having been put right, brought into order, and improved that things become truly useful.

Confucius was possessed of an extremely persuasive eloquence that we, who have only the written record of his teachings, can barely imagine. It was not only the content of his speech but also his extraordinary confidence conveyed through the very sound of his voice and his calm rhythms. Gradually, as young Zilu stood before him, all signs of rebellion disappeared from his demeanor, and he began to listen to the sage with respect and attentiveness.

"However, sir," Zilu then said, for he had not yet lost the energy to counter-question, "it is said that the bamboos of South Mountain grow naturally straight, though unattended to, and if one cuts a piece of bamboo and uses it as a spear, it can pierce even the hide of a rhinoceros. If so, what need for learning is there for a naturally gifted man?"

For Confucius, nothing was easier than knocking holes in such a simple-minded comparison. "If you take this piece of bamboo from South Mountain that you speak of and attach feathers to one end and an arrowhead to the other, and polish and improve it, this piece of bamboo can do far more than pierce the hide of a rhinoceros."

When the admirably pure-hearted Zilu heard these words, he was at a loss. His face flushed; apparently he had been made to think hard. Abruptly he tossed the rooster and the pig aside and bowed his head in surrender: "May I humbly request your instruction, sir?" It was not only that Zilu could find no apt rejoinder. The truth was that, meeting Confucius and listening to him, Zilu knew that this was no place for a rooster or a pig; and he was overcome by the vastness of the gap between himself and the man before him.

That very day, Zilu formally paid reverence to Confucius as his teacher and became his disciple.

Two

Zilu had never before met anyone like Confucius. He had seen a champion strong enough to lift a copper vessel weighing thousands of kilograms, and he had heard of a sage who could observe occurrences a thousand leagues distant. But what Confucius possessed was quite different from such monstrously abnormal powers: It was common sense brought to a pitch of perfection. He had taken his gifts of intellect, emotion, and will, as well as his physical abilities, and developed them splendidly, in a way that was at once ordinary and exemplary. For the first time Zilu witnessed a richness of spirit in which each excellence was in perfect balance, without lack or excess, so that it remained inconspicuous. He saw with wonder how spontaneous and free Confucius was, without a trace of the constraints of a professional sage. Zilu felt immediately that this man had lived a hard life. And, curiously, Confucius was superior to Zilu in physical prowess as well, including the martial arts in which the youth took such pride, although the older man refrained from relying on them in daily life. This surprised Zilu, who was, as we have said, a chivalrous ronin.

Confucius had keen psychological insight into all manner of persons, so much so that Zilu wondered if the Master had not, at some point, led a wild and dissolute life. His knowledge was as broad as it was practical, and it also embraced the highest, purest idealism. Clearly, the Master was one who, judged by standards most worldly and most rigorously ethical, could manage well in any situation. Up to this point, the excellence of anyone Zilu had encountered lay always in their usefulness:

They were "good for" some purpose or another. But that was not the case with Confucius. It was enough that such a person as he should exist—so it seemed to Zilu, who, completely taken with the Master, felt, after less than a month as his disciple, that he could not survive without his spiritual support.

In the long, painful cycle of wanderings that made up the latter years of Confucius' life, no one was as devoted to the Master as Zilu. It was not because he hoped being his disciple would gain him official employment; nor, oddly enough, was it because he hoped to cultivate his virtue and talent. No, it was a pure feeling of veneration, which sought nothing for itself and remained unchanged until death, that kept Zilu at the Master's side. In the past he had never allowed himself to be parted from his sword, and now he felt the same about this man.

Confucius was not yet forty years old—the age of which he famously said: "At forty, the gentleman is no longer unsure of his way." He was only nine years older than Zilu. Yet the difference to Zilu seemed infinite.

Confucius, for his part, was surprised at how difficult it was to train this particular disciple. He had encountered any number of men who were smitten with notions of valor and who disliked mildness; but it was unusual to find someone so contemptuous of proper form as was Zilu. Although one must ultimately rely on spirit, propriety and rites needed to be approached through form. This principle, of "approaching through form," was not something Zilu could accept. He willingly accepted that "'Rites' refers to the spirit of the Rites. How could it refer merely to the decorative cloth used when presenting gems? 'Music' refers to the spirit of Music. How could it refer merely to bells and drums?" But when the actual details of propriety and decorum were discussed, Zilu grew bored. Teaching someone so instinctively averse to formalism the nature of Rites and Music was no easy task, even for Confucius.

But it was still more difficult for Zilu to learn such lessons. It was Confucius' own richness of spirit that Zilu relied upon, but it was inconceivable to Zilu that such richness of spirit could result from the accumulation of specific precise actions in Confucius' daily life. Zilu claimed that first must come the root, and then the branches—principles, and then practice—but he was forever being scolded by Confucius for not having given thought to the question of how to cultivate that initial root. His veneration for Confucius was unquestionable, but adopting the Master's views without question was another matter.

When Confucius said that the very wise and the very foolish are hard to change, he did not have Zilu in mind, for the Master did not consider Zilu to be very foolish, despite his many faults. In fact, he had the highest regard for his bold and reckless disciple's extraordinary virtue: namely, his pure disinterestedness. This was a quality rare among the people of the land, and, in fact, no one apart from Confucius considered this a virtue in Zilu; on the contrary, it was seen as incomprehensible foolishness. Confucius alone was aware that Zilu's valor and political skills were as nothing compared to this most remarkable kind of foolishness. Only with regard to his parents was Zilu able to do as the Master urged, which was to restrain himself and to follow proper form at all cost. This became the talk of his relatives—how the wild Zilu had, after studying under Confucius, become a filial son. It seemed odd to Zilu, being praised like that. Far from being a filial son, he could not repress the feeling that he was living falsely. He had been true to himself when he was insisting on having his own way and driving his parents to distraction. He felt a little sorry for his parents now, so easily pleased were they with his deceptive conduct. Zilu was not an insightful student of human psychology, but he was extremely straightforward—and from such straightforwardness this awareness arose. Many years later, noticing one day how his parents had aged and recalling how fine and healthy they were when he was a child, Zilu burst into tears. From that time forward, his filial behavior became so self-sacrificial that it was without peer; but before then, his sudden conversion to filial piety was as described above.

Three

As Zilu was going for a walk in town one day, he ran into a few former friends. If they were not quite ruffians, they were certainly rough, unscrupulous ronin-types. One of them stared at the robe Zilu was wearing and said, "So this is what they call a scholar's gown? Damn shabby, if you ask me. And say, don't tell me you don't miss your sword!" Zilu ignored this. Then the former friend said something that Zilu could not ignore: "How about it? People have been saying that teacher Kong Qiu is a hypocrite. Preaching away with that priggish look on his face, trying to make people believe what he doesn't believe himself. What a way to make a sweet living for yourself!"

The man had not spoken with any particular malice; it was just his careless way of badmouthing others. But Zilu turned deep red. He grabbed the man by the collar, punched him in the face, once, twice, three times, and then let go. The man fell to the ground, stunned. As if issuing a challenge, Zilu glared angrily at the others, who were dumbfounded; but they knew how strong and brave Zilu was, and they did not make a move. They helped their fallen friend up, and left without a word.

At some point news of this incident reached Confucius. Zilu was summoned and, when he presented himself to the Master, was made to listen to what follows:

"The gentlemen of ancient times made fidelity their essential character, and benevolence their protection. When something wrong was done, they rectified it through fidelity; when attacks on them were made, they defended themselves through benevolence. This is why they saw no need for physical force. Now the petty man tends to regard arrogance as bravery, but the bravery of a gentleman consists in establishing justice."

Zilu listened respectfully.

Some days later, Zilu was going for a walk again when he heard a group of idlers arguing on a tree-shaded street. They seemed to be talking about Confucius: "'In the old days, in the old days'—he's always dragging in talk of the old days to criticize the present. Well, no one's seen the old days, so you can say whatever you like about them, can't you now? If you could rule the country just by following the old ways according to the rules, anybody could do it! You've got to have respect for a crafty politician like Yang Hu. At least he's alive, not like the noble duke of Zhou, who's been dead a long time."

These were times of social disorder. Political power had passed from the Marquis of Lu to his minister, Ji Sun; and it was now about to pass from Ji Sun to the ambitious Yang Hu, who was a retainer of Ji Sun's. The man holding forth may well have been a relative of this Yang Hu. He went on:

"Yang Hu sent a bunch of messengers to Kong Qiu, asking him to join the government. But incredibly Kong Qiu said he didn't want to serve in the government! That guy talks a good game, but when it comes to real live politics, you find out he's all talk and no show."

Zilu pushed his way through the onlookers and went up to the old man. Everyone realized immediately that Zilu was a disciple of Confucius. The old man, once so sure of himself, turned pale, lowered his head, and shrank back into the crowd. He had seen the expression on Zilu's face, his eyes flashing with righteous indignation.

This same kind of interchange was replayed in various situations. So, whenever the figure of Zilu appeared in the distance, shoulders heaving and eyes ablaze, people refrained from slanderous comments about Confucius. Zilu was admonished by the Master regarding this several times, but Zilu was unable to act differently. He was not entirely without excuse, in his own mind at least. It went something like this:

"If a gentleman, as they call him, feels the same degree of anger as I do and is still able to restrain himself, why, that is splendid! But a gentleman would not feel as angry as I do; no, his convictions are weak enough that he can contain them. Of that, I am sure."

After a year had passed, Confucius, with a pained smile, lamented: "Since Zilu entered my gates, I have stopped hearing any criticism of me whatsoever!"

Four

One day Zilu was playing the zither. In the next room Confucius listened, and after a while he turned to the disciple Ranyou, who was sitting beside him, and said: "Listen to the sound of that zither! Is it not filled with wildness and passion? The sounds produced by a gentleman must be mild and moderate, cultivating the spirit of growth. Anciently, Shun played the five-stringed zither and composed the Song of the South Wind:

> *Fragrant is the south wind—*
> *With it, we can resolve the anger of our people.*
> *Now is the time of the south wind—*
> *With it, we can increase the wealth of our people.*

If you listen to Zilu's playing, the sense is violent and extreme. It is not the sound of the south, it is the voice of the north. Never has there been anything that reflected so sharply the willful, irresponsible spirit of the player."

Later, Ranyou went to Zilu and reported Confucius' remark. Zilu knew that he had little innate talent for music, and he had thought his ears and fingers to be at fault. Learning that, in fact, the problem was more profound, relating to his spiritual state, surprised and frightened him. Manual practice was not most important, then: he needed to think about things more deeply. He retreated to his room to fast and to meditate. After several days, during which time he grew so thin one could see his bones, he believed he had come to understand what was wrong, and took up his zither once again. With trepidation he began to play. In the next room Confucius listened for a while but said nothing; nor did his face show any sign of displeasure. The disciple Zigong went to Zilu and told him this, and Zilu smiled with happiness at the news that the Master was not displeased.

Seeing the smile on the face of the good-natured Zilu, the clever Zigong, who was the younger disciple, could not repress a quiet smile of his own. Zigong understood the situation well: Zilu's playing of the zither was still full of the wildness of the north, and if Confucius did not censure him for it, this was simply because he felt pity for Zilu, so utterly intent on moderating his playing that he had grown gaunt through worry.

Five

Among the disciples of Confucius, none was scolded as frequently by the Master as Zilu, and none dared counter-question the Master so boldly as he. "Respectfully I ask, may one abandon the Way of the ancients and follow one's own inclinations?" he would venture, although it was obvious that the notion would be rebuked. Or he would come right out with a response on the order of "How roundabout you are in your way of teaching, sir!" No one else would dare to say such a thing. Yet there was also no one who was as thoroughly dependent upon Confucius as this same Zilu. If he kept on questioning their teacher, it was because Zilu was the kind of man who could not pretend to agree to something he was not really convinced of, and because, unlike the other disciples, he did not worry whether he would be laughed at or scolded.

Precisely because Zilu was a free and independent man who was generally unwilling to subordinate himself to anyone else, a high-spirited fellow whose word was his bond, the way in which he attended Confucius like an ordinary disciple created an odd impression. And in fact he had a slightly comical tendency to be completely at ease, leaving all complex thoughts and important decisions to the Master, but only when he was actually with him. He was like a small child who, in the presence of his mother, is content to have her do everything—including things he can manage for himself. So much so that Zilu himself sometimes smiled wryly when he stepped back and thought about his behavior.

And yet there was something deep within Zilu that not even his respected master was allowed to touch upon: a line drawn that no one could cross. That is to say, there was something of supreme importance to Zilu in this world, in the face of which even life and death were not worth considering, much less matters of gain or loss. If we call it "chivalry," it would seem too light; and if we call it "fidelity" or "justice," it would seem too moralistic, too lacking in a fine, free, active spirit. So let us not worry about what to call it—to Zilu, it was a kind of pleasure. Whatever was accompanied by this feeling was good, and whatever was not was bad. This was utterly clear to him, and he had never had occasion to doubt. It was rather different from what Confucius referred to as "benevolence," but Zilu chose to adopt from among the Master's teachings only those elements that would complement this simplistic ethical view of his:

"Using fine words, ingratiating looks, and excessive courtesy to hide one's resentment and to pretend friendship—all this I regard as shameful." And: "One must not do injury to benevolence for the sake of one's life; one should perfect benevolence even at the cost of one's life." And again: "The zealous man actively pursues the truth, and the prudent man will hold back from doing wrong."

Confucius at first tried to correct this fault of Zilu's but eventually gave up, recalling the proverb that warned against "straightening a bull's horns at the cost of killing the bull"—recognizing that Zilu was, after all, a splendid bull of a man. Some disciples required a whip to get them moving, while others needed a rope to tether them. Confucius understood that the same personality defects that made Zilu so hard to control with a simple tether were at the same time traits that could be of great use. It would be enough to give Zilu an indication of the general direction to go in:

"To be respectful yet fail to observe propriety is to be coarse; to be valiant yet fail to observe propriety is to go against the Way." And: "To be fond of fidelity but not of learning is to risk injury to others; to be fond of directness but not of learning is to risk narrowness." Language like this was for the most part directed at Zilu not as an individual but in his capacity as the head student, for characteristics that could be attractive in Zilu personally often became defects in his many fellow students.

Six

It is said that, in the Weiyu region of Jin, stones began to speak. In the view of one wise observer, the resentment of the people was expressing itself through the stones. The already weakened House of Zhou had divided into two factions at odds with each other. Over ten large states kept allying with, then fighting against one another, and wars never ceased. A marquis of Qi had an affair with the wife of a minister, stealing into her chambers every night, but was discovered and killed by the husband. In the state of Chu a member of the royal family strangled the king on his sickbed and thus gained the throne. In Wu criminals who had been punished by having their feet chopped off attacked the king; in Jin two ministers of state exchanged wives. That was the kind of world it was.

Duke Zhao of Lu attacked Ji Pingzi but found himself driven out of his own domain. Although the possibility of his return emerged, the retainers who followed him into exile were afraid of their fate, and so they kept the duke in foreign exile until he died in poverty seven years later. Lu went from being controlled by the three clans of Ji Sun, Shu Sun, and Meng Sun to being entirely at the mercy of Yang Hu, a retainer of the Ji clan.

No sooner had Yang Hu, the strategist, been tripped up by his own strategies, however, than the political winds in the land of Lu shifted. Quite unexpectedly, Confucius was appointed mayor of the town of Zhongdu. Since this was a period when fair-minded, selfless civil servants were few, and most officials devoted themselves to exacting taxes from the populace for personal gain, the just policies and meticulous planning of Confucius produced astonishing results in a very short time. The ruler, Duke Ding, filled with admiration, asked: "Would it be possible to rule the whole land of Lu using the methods you have used in Zhongdu?" Confucius responded: "Why only Lu? One could rule the whole empire in such ways." Now Duke Ding was even more astonished, since Confucius, who was a stranger to boasting of any kind, had spoken so boldly, although calmly and respectfully. The duke without delay appointed Confucius as the official in charge of land and civil affairs, then to a yet higher post as the official in charge of law enforcement, the judiciary, and general administration—in short, Confucius was chief minister.

Upon the recommendation of Confucius, Zilu was named an official attached to the Ji clan, equivalent to being chief secretary to the cabinet of Lu. As such, he was instrumental in the enactment of the governmental reforms proposed by the Master. The first of Confucius' policies was centralization of power, that is, strengthening the authority of the ruler of Lu. To achieve this, the power of the three clans of Ji, Shu, and Meng, who actually exercised more influence than the duke himself, needed to be diminished. The three clans each lived in private fortresses, at Hou, Fei, and Cheng, whose walls were nine meters thick and three meters high. Confucius decided that these fortresses should be destroyed, and the task was entrusted to Zilu.

For a man like Zilu, to see the results of his labors immediately, unequivocally, and on a scale far larger than he had ever experienced, was an undeniable gratification. In particular, to smash the evil organizations and customs that powerful politicians had spread throughout the land gave him a sense of purpose he had not known before. And he was happy to see Confucius' face as the Master devoted his energies to the attainment of these long-cherished goals. Confucius, for his part, had full confidence in Zilu not simply as one of his disciples but as an able politician.

At Fei, however, the duke's forces were met by a revolt led by Gongshan Buniu, which then proceeded to attack the capital of Lu. At one point, the situation became so dire that the arrows of the rebel army landed close to Duke Ding, who had fled to Wuzitai; but disaster was averted, if barely, through Confucius' intelligent tactical decisions. Zilu was impressed anew with the Master's abilities as a practical man of affairs. He had seen how physically strong he was, and how skilled at politics, but he had never dreamed how brilliant his master would be in directing an army in actual battle. Of course, Zilu himself fought at the forefront of the battle, and he derived a certain pleasure from wielding his sword again after such a long hiatus. At any rate, it was more in keeping with Zilu's character to contend with the rough realities of life than to study the classics or absorb the forms of ancient etiquette.

In order to conclude a humiliating peace with Qi, Duke Ding met with Duke Jing of Qi at Xiagu, bringing Confucius along with him. Duke Jing—and his lords and ministers—were the victors, but Confucius took the offensive, criticizing them mercilessly for their lack of courtesy; it was said that Duke Jing and his entourage were left trembling. Hearing this, Zilu was overjoyed. But the powerful state of Qi now grew fearful of Confucius as chief minister of their neighbor, and of the strength of Lu, which was increasing as a result of his policies. After much deliberation, they decided on a desperate measure that was typical of ancient China. A troupe of beautiful young women accomplished in song and dance was dispatched as a gift to the ruler of Lu, with the goal of weakening the will of the duke of Lu and driving a wedge between him and Confucius. And still more typical of ancient China, this crude stratagem, coupled with actions by the anti-Confucius faction within Lu, had almost instant success. Duke Ding was seduced into giving himself over to the company of the dancers and stopped attending to the business of court. From Ji Huanzi on down, the high officials soon followed their ruler's example. Zilu was furious; he clashed with the officials and resigned his post. Confucius did not give up so quickly, seeking still to improve the situation. Zilu was anxious for the Master to resign—not because he feared Confucius would do anything unworthy of a faithful minister, but because he could not bear that the Master should be in the midst of such licentiousness.

So when at last, despite his tenacity, Confucius abandoned his efforts and resigned his position, Zilu was relieved. When the Master left the land of Lu, Zilu gladly followed. With the capital receding into the distance, Confucius, a poet and composer, began to sing: "Even the gentleman must flee before the sweet words of a beautiful woman; even the gentleman may be brought down by the flattery of a beautiful woman."

Thus began the long wanderings of Confucius.

Seven

Zilu had one great doubt. It had been with him in childhood, and even now that he was a man, almost on the brink of old age, the doubt continued to plague him—far more than anyone else. It focused on the commonplace fact that evil often flourishes and righteousness is made to suffer.

Whenever he encountered this situation, Zilu could not repress deep feelings of sorrow and anger. How can this be? People seemed to concede that evil might prosper for a time, but in the end there would be just retribution. Of course that might occur, but would that not merely confirm the truth that human beings were doomed? As for justice finally triumphing, Zilu could not remember an instance of that happening in the present day, whatever might have been the case in ancient times. So why? What was the reason for this sad state of affairs? The indignation of Zilu, the grown-up child, was infinite. He almost found himself stamping his foot, as he contemplated these questions: "What is this Heaven people talk about? Doesn't Heaven see what is going on? And if Heaven decides men's fate like this, how am I supposed to keep from rebelling against it? Does Heaven fail to distinguish between the good and the bad, just as it ignores the distinction between men and beasts? Is everything—even righteousness and wickedness—relative, with man alone the measure of all things?"

When Zilu took these questions to Confucius, the response was always the same: a lecture on the true nature of human happiness. So the only reward for doing good was the satisfaction that comes from knowing one has done good? Was that it?

When he was in the presence of his teacher, Zilu felt he could accept this; but when he was by himself again, a lingering dissatisfaction returned. He could not accept a happiness that was the result of such forced reasoning. Without a clear, universally acknowledged reward for the good and the just, it would not do.

Zilu's dissatisfaction with the ways of Heaven was especially sharp when he considered the circumstances of Confucius. Why should a man who was of almost superhuman ability and virtue have to submit to a life of obscurity? He had not even been blessed with domestic happiness. Why should such a man have to endure the misfortune of leading a wanderer's life in his old age? One night he listened as Confucius muttered to himself: "The Phoenix does not come. The River does not yield up the Wonder Horse with the auspicious signs upon its back. All is lost!" Zilu could not hold back his tears. Confucius' lament was for all the people of the world, but Zilu was crying for Confucius alone.

Zilu considered this man, his teacher, and the world in which he had to live, and Zilu wept. And he resolved: From this day forward he would make of himself a shield to protect this man from all assaults of the defiled world. In return for Confucius' spiritual guidance, he would take upon himself every worldly trial and humiliation. Presumptuous though it might seem, he felt it his duty. When it came to learning, Zilu might be inferior to more talented junior disciples; but in time of need, he before anyone else would gladly cast aside his life for the Master. Of that he had no doubt.

Eight

"Here is a beautiful jewel! Shall we hide it in a casket? Shall we seek a merchant to sell it to?" When Zigong asked this, Confucius at once replied, "Sell it, sell it! But wait for a good price."

In this spirit Confucius set out on his travels throughout the land. The disciples who accompanied him were eager to "sell" themselves, but Zilu felt differently. From his recent experience as an official in Lu, he knew how gratifying it was to be in a position with the power to carry out one's convictions; but in that case it was the privilege of working under the direction of Confucius that had been critical. Without that, it would be better to live "wearing coarse clothing while hiding one's jewel within one's bosom." If he had to spend his life serving as a guard dog for the Master, he would have no regrets. He was not without worldly ambition, but to be a mediocre official would go against his natural temperament, which was frank and open-hearted.

Among the disciples accompanying Confucius in his travels were all kinds of men: the business-like Ranyou; the warm-hearted elder Min Zichian; the inquisitive Zixia, an expert in the customs of ancient times; the hedonistic Zaiyu, inclined toward sophistry; the strong-minded Gongliang Ru, a harsh critic of the times; simple, straightforward Zigao, a man so small he was only half as tall as Confucius, whose height was said to be nearly three meters. But as regards both age and dignity, Zilu was their unquestioned chief.

Although twenty-two years younger than Zilu, Zigong possessed remarkable abilities, and Zilu hoped for Zigong's advancement rather than Yanhui's. Yanhui was always being praised to the skies by the Master, and other disciples, including Zigong and Zizhang, could not help feeling envious. Not Zilu, however—he was too senior to feel envy, and besides, Zilu was not given to such feelings. Even so, he could see little merit in Yanhui's capacity for receptiveness and flexibility. The young man seemed a faint shadow of Confucius, without the political sense and vitality of the Master, and Zilu could not abide that.

Zigong, who was clever and active, if a bit shallow, was more to Zilu's taste. Nor was Zilu alone in appreciating Zigong's perspicacity. Anyone could see that his character was not as well developed as his mind, but then, he was still young. Upon occasion, Zilu would be so upset by Zigong's frivolity that he shouted at him; but, for the most part, he felt awe at the thought of how far Zigong would be able to advance in time.

Here was an example of Zigong's thinking, which he dared to express to a few fellow disciples: "People say that the Master dislikes eloquence, but I think he himself is too eloquent, and this requires that we be on our guard. For example, his eloquence is entirely unlike Zaiyu's skill in speech, which is so apparent that it may give pleasure to the listener but does not carry real conviction. And that is why there is no danger in it. The Master's speech is something quite different. In place of fluency, it has a weight that leaves no room for doubt on the part of the listener. In place of wit, it has richly nuanced metaphors that no one can resist. Of course I know that ninety-nine percent of what the Master says is unquestionably true, and that ninety-nine percent of what he does serves as a model for us all. Still, that other one percent—that mere one percent of the Master's always persuasive eloquence—might at times be used to excuse the minute portion of the Master's character that is not fully in accord with absolute, universal truth. And this is where we must be careful! It may be that I am too close to the Master, too accustomed to him, and that is why I say this. Certainly, if later generations venerate the Master as a sage, nothing could be more natural. I have never seen a person so close to perfection as he, and such men will rarely appear in the future. All I mean to suggest is that the Master, too, has qualities, however minute, that require us to exercise caution. I am sure that someone as similar in temperament to the Master as Yanhui does not feel any of the dissatisfaction that I am feeling. It is that similarity of temperament that causes the Master to praise Yanhui so often."

Zilu was annoyed that Zigong, greenhorn that he was, should presume to criticize the Master; he knew that ultimately it was jealousy of Yanhui that made him speak as he did. Still, the purport of Zigong's observations could not be so easily dismissed. And as regards the matter of similarities and differences in temperament, Zilu himself had some thoughts of his own. Admiring Zigong's insight but having contempt for his brashness, Zilu concluded: "This cheeky kid has a gift for saying clearly what the rest of us are only vaguely aware of."

In discussion, Zigong once posed this curious question to Confucius: "Do the dead know what we do, or do they not?" The reference was to the presence or absence of consciousness after death, to the mortality or immortality of the soul. Confucius gave this curious reply: "If I say that the dead know, I fear that filial sons and grandsons will make the funeral rites so elaborate that they will be a detriment to their own livelihood. If I say that the dead do not know, I fear that unfilial children will abandon the bodies of their parents without bothering about funeral rites."

Zigong thought this answer irrelevant and unsatisfactory. The Master well understood the meaning of his disciple's question; but, realist that he was, and placing prime emphasis on everyday life as he always did, Confucius sought to shift the direction of this promising disciple's question.

Zigong went to Zilu and reported this discussion. Zilu had no particular interest in the question of the survival of consciousness, but now his curiosity was piqued. One day he asked Confucius about death. This was the Master's reply: "We do not yet know about life. How then could we know about death?"

"Absolutely right!" Zilu said, full of admiration. When he told Zigong about this, Zigong once again felt that the question had just been deftly sidestepped, and the expression on his face seemed to say: "No doubt that is so, but I was asking about something quite different."

Nine

Duke Ling of Wei was a weak-willed ruler. He was not so stupid as to confuse the wise with the talentless; still, he valued sweet words of flattery more than admonitions that were painful to hear.

The policies of Wei were controlled from the women's quarters of the palace. The duke's wife, Lady Nanzi, had long been known for her licentiousness. When she was a princess in the land of Song, she indulged in intimate relations with her half-brother Chao, who was famous for his good looks; and after she married Duke Ling, she invited Chao to join the Wei court as a high official so she might resume their immoral relationship. She was a talented woman and often interfered in political matters; whatever she indicated, Duke Ling agreed to. Anyone who wished to gain the duke's ear had first to curry favor with her.

When Confucius moved from Lu to Wei, he presented himself, as commanded, for an audience with the duke, but he did not pay his respects to Lady Nanzi. This displeased her greatly. She immediately dispatched a courier to Confucius with the message: "All gentlemen who wish to enjoy fraternal relations with the Sovereign seek an audience with his Consort. Lady Nanzi wishes you to seek an audience with her."

So Confucius was compelled to pay his respects to her. When Lady Nanzi received him, she was sitting behind a gauzy curtain. Confucius bowed gravely to her as she sat to the north, as was customary for a ruler; and as she returned his bow, we are told, the jewels attached to her sash tinkled gently.

When Confucius got back from the ducal palace, Zilu's unhappiness was undisguised. He had hoped that the Master would simply ignore a demand from the likes of Lady Nanzi. Of course he knew that Confucius could never be seduced by a jezebel like her, but it distressed him that someone as pure and incorrupt as the Master should have bowed to such a defiled, lewd woman. He felt like one who treasures a beautiful piece of jade and cannot bear to have even the shadow of impurity fall upon its surface. Confucius, for his part, was both amused and troubled to observe that the "grown-up child" who dwelt alongside the able man of affairs within Zilu showed no signs of maturing.

One day not long after, a courier delivered a message that the duke wished to discuss various matters with the Master while taking a tour of the capital by carriage. Highly pleased, Confucius dressed properly for the occasion and set out at once.

Lady Nanzi, however, was not at all happy that Duke Ling venerated this tall, brusque old man as a sage. Further, it was outrageous that she should be cavalierly brushed aside so that the two of them might ride about the capital together in a carriage.

Confucius had his audience with the duke and was about to step into the carriage after him when Lady Nanzi was discovered to be already seated in it, gorgeously attired. There was no space for Confucius. Lady Nanzi turned to the duke with a mean little smile. Uncomfortable at the situation, Confucius looked coolly toward the duke, who looked down in embarrassment. He said nothing to Lady Nanzi, and silently motioned that Confucius should get into a second carriage.

The entourage began its tour of the capital of Wei. In front was the splendid, horse-drawn, four-wheeled carriage in which the glamorous figure of Lady Nanzi sat alongside Duke Ling; she was as radiant as a peony in full bloom. Following was the shabby, ox-drawn, two-wheeled carriage in which a solitary Confucius sat, his posture erect, facing straight ahead. Among the crowds that lined the streets, there were murmurs and signs of disapproval.

Zilu, who was mingling with the crowds, took all this in. Having seen the pleasure of the Master when the invitation arrived from the duke, Zilu was now infuriated. As Lady Nanzi passed before him, squealing with delight at something or other, Zilu's hands formed into fists. He pushed through the throng, preparing to leap out at her, but he felt hands pulling him back. Trying to shake himself free, Zilu turned around, eyes blazing with anger.

It was Ziruo and Zizheng, his fellow disciples. As they held onto his sleeve, there were tears in their eyes. Finally Zilu's hands fell to his sides.

The next day, Confucius and his group left Wei. On this occasion, this was the Master's lament: "I have never seen a man who is as fond of virtue as he is of pleasure."

Ten

Shegong, informally known as Zigao, was extremely fond of dragons. He had dragons carved on the walls of his room and dragons painted on his tapestries: he spent his days surrounded by images of dragons. A heavenly dragon, pleased to hear of this, descended on Shegong's house one day to see this admirer of dragons. The heavenly dragon was wondrously large, and as its tail wound itself around the hall its head peered into the window. Shegong caught sight of it, began to tremble, and fled in fright. He was such a coward that his face lost all its color, and his very soul deserted him.

The various rulers of China were fond of the idea of Confucius as a sage, but they did not care for the reality of his wisdom. They were like Shegong with regard to dragons. The actual Confucius was far too large a presence. There were rulers who treated him as an official Guest of State, and there were those who employed his disciples. There was no ruler, however, who attempted to put into practice the Master's policies. In Kuang Confucius was subjected to humiliation by a violent mob; in Song he was persecuted by wicked officials; and in Pu he was again attacked by a band of ruffians. All that seemed to await him was polite distancing by rulers, envy by government-appointed scholars, and exclusion by politicians.

And still Confucius continued to lecture and to work to perfect himself as he and his disciples traveled tirelessly from state to state. "A bird chooses the tree on which to perch. How can the tree choose the bird?" he would say, keeping up his spirits; but he never became cynical and sought always to be of use. He sincerely believed, incredible though it may seem, that his desire to be employed by a ruler was not for his sake but for the sake of the world, and of the Way. Optimistic even in poverty and hopeful even in adversity—truly, it was an uncommon group of men.

Once, Confucius and his disciples were invited for an audience with King Zhao of Chu. The ministers of the states of Chen and Cai, afraid that Chu might employ him, conspired to have a band of thugs descend upon the group as they approached the city. It was not the first time the group had been so attacked, but it was the most dangerous.

Supplies were exhausted, and the group was without proper food for seven days. Hungry and weak, many fell ill. In the midst of hardship and fear, the Master alone lost none of his vitality; he played the zither and he sang as he usually did. Zilu, who could not bear to see the plight of his fellow disciples, approached Confucius, his face flushed slightly with anger. Was it in accord with propriety for the Master to sing at a time like this? The Master did not reply, but continued to pluck the strings of the zither. Then, when the song was finished, he replied: "Zilu, I say to you: The gentleman delights in music in order to do away with arrogance. The petty man delights in music in order to calm his fears. Who is this who would follow me, yet does not know me?"

Zilu could not believe his ears. To speak of playing music in order to eliminate arrogance—in a terrible situation like this? But suddenly he realized what Confucius meant, and he was overcome with joy; he picked up a spear and started to dance. The Master accompanied him on the zither, repeating the melody three times. The disciples gave themselves over to enjoyment of this rustic improvised dance, and forgot for a while their hunger and fatigue.

Zilu, surveying the difficult circumstances of the group, then asked Confucius: "Is the gentleman ever perplexed?" He asked this because he believed that, according to the Master's doctrine, this could never be the case. Confucius' reply was immediate: "Does 'perplexed' not mean to be perplexed about the Way? At present, I am clinging to the Way of Benevolence and Righteousness and meet with suffering in this disordered world. Why should I be considered to be perplexed? If 'perplexed' means hunger and fatigue, then the gentleman, too, can of course be perplexed. However, when the petty man is perplexed, he exceeds all bounds."

That is the difference, Confucius was saying. Zilu found himself flushed again, this time in shame, feeling as if the petty man within him had been exposed. Watching Confucius, who knew that distress was a matter of fate and so was not upset by calamity, Zilu was overcome by the Master's great heroism.

By comparison, how small and mean was the heroism of facing, without blinking, the sword of an opponent, in which he had previously taken such pride.

Eleven

On the way from Xiu to She, Zilu lagged behind the rest of the group. He was walking alone through a field when he encountered an old man carrying a bamboo basket. Zilu casually greeted him and asked if he had not perhaps seen the Master pass by. The old man answered gruffly: "'Master, Master,' you say, but how should I know who you mean by that?" The old man looked Zilu over, then laughed contemptuously: "You seem like the kind of man who does no work and spends the day idly thinking and arguing." Without so much as a backward glance, the old man walked off and began hacking at weeds. He must be a hermit, thought Zilu, bowing slightly and remaining where he was, waiting to be spoken to again. The old man worked silently for a while, then returned to Zilu and guided him to his home.

The sun was beginning to set. The old man killed a chicken and boiled some millet for supper; then he introduced his two sons to Zilu. After the meal, feeling the effects of the cloudy rice wine, the old man picked up a zither and started to pluck the strings. His sons sang along:

There is plenty of dew, which won't dry until the sun shines:
Relaxing in our cups tonight, we won't stop until we're drunk!

Unquestionably, these were poor people, and yet their home over-
flowed with a relaxed happiness and spiritual richness. Nor did Zilu
fail to see occasional intelligent flashes in the expressions of the three
men, filled with amiability as they were.

Putting down his zither, the old man turned to Zilu and said: "To
travel by land, one needs a cart, and to travel by water, a boat. This has
been true since ancient times. What would you think of someone who
tried to travel by land using a boat? That would be like trying to apply
the ancient laws of Zhou to the present world! If you clothe a monkey
in the robes of the duke of Zhou, it will tear them right off."

As he went on in this vein, it was obvious that the old man knew
Zilu was a follower of Confucius. "Only when you have made yourself
perfectly comfortable and happy can you be said to be successful. It is
not a matter of having the cap or carriage of an official." Perfect tran-
quillity was apparently the old man's ideal. This was not the first time
Zilu had encountered the philosophy of retirement, for he had already
met Changzu and Jieni, as well as Jieyu, the feigned madman of Chu.
But Zilu had not entered into their daily life nor spent an entire evening with them. As he listened to the gentle words of the old man and
observed his easy manner, Zilu thought that this, too, was a beautiful
way of life, and even felt a little envious of it.

Nevertheless, he did not simply listen to the old man's words in silence. This is what he said to the three men: "Of course it must be comfortable to cut off all connection with the world, but securing perfect
comfort is not what makes a person truly human. To seek to please one's
own small self while ignoring grand moral principles is not the proper
Way of Man. Our group realized long ago that the Way was not going to
be practiced in the world as it is now. We also realized that it is dangerous
to preach the Way at present. But precisely because it is a world without
the Way, it is necessary to preach the Way, despite risk to ourselves."

The next morning Zilu departed from the old man's home and

hurried along the path. As he walked, he found himself comparing the lives of Confucius and the old man. Of course Confucius' insight was not a whit inferior to the old man's, nor were his worldly attachments any greater. But even so, Confucius had put aside any effort to make himself perfectly comfortable and happy and instead traversed the land for the sake of the Way. As he considered this, Zilu felt a dislike for the old man that he had not experienced at all the night before. Close to noon, he caught a glimpse of Confucius and his disciples far ahead, on a road that passed through a deep green field of barley. When he got close enough to see the exceedingly tall figure of Confucius, Zilu suddenly felt something akin to pain constricting his chest.

Twelve

As they rode the ferry from Song to Chen, Zigong and Zaiyu were having a discussion about Confucius' claim: "In a hamlet of ten households, there would certainly be someone like me in regards to loyalty and fidelity. But there would be no one as fond of learning." Zigong argued that, despite these words, the Master's wondrous perfection was due to the extraordinary nature of his inborn gifts. Zaiyu, on the other hand, said that the Master's conscious efforts to perfect himself were the larger factor, that the gap between the abilities of Confucius and his disciples was quantitative rather than qualitative. What Confucius had, the mass of men also had. But the Master had, by constantly taking pains, brought each quality to its present state of perfection—that was the only difference. Zigong responded that if a quantitative difference was overwhelming, it became in effect a qualitative difference. Besides, the Master's ability to maintain a constant effort at self-perfection was in itself proof of the heaven-bestowed extraordinariness of his nature, was it not? Yet the most central thing by far in Confucius' genius was, Zigong averred, his splendid instinctive sense of the Mean, which made his every action beautiful, in all times and circumstances.

"Ah, listen to them talk!" thought Zilu as he sat to one side with a cranky expression on his face. "All talk and no guts. If this boat overturned right now, their faces would turn white with panic. In an emergency, I'm the only one who could be of real help to the Master!" Looking at the two able young talkers, he recalled the saying that "fine words often impede virtue"; he felt glad to be able to trust in the purity of his own heart.

And yet Zilu himself was not entirely free of dissatisfaction with the Master. After Duke Ling of Chen committed adultery with the wife of one of his vassals, and went to the audience chamber at court one morning wearing her undergarment, making sure that all would see, a retainer named Xieye admonished the duke and was killed for his forthrightness. A disciple asked Confucius about this incident from about a century before. Xieye's righteous remonstrance and subsequent execution seemed like the admonitory death of the famous vassal Bigan in ancient times. Could one call it a display of Benevolence? The Master replied that, no, Bigan and King Zhou were related by blood; moreover, Bigan held a very high official rank. That was why he could expect that, after he had risked everything and been executed as a result, King Zhou would soon repent. This could indeed be called Benevolence. But in the case of Xieye and Duke Ling, there were no ties of blood, and Xieye's rank was low. Knowing that "If the ruler is unrighteous, the state is unrighteous," he should have withdrawn himself. Yet, forgetful of his station, he tried to rectify the wickedness of an entire country with his own petty person. He threw away his life in vain. His actions by no means rose to the level of Benevolence.

The disciple who had raised the question seemed satisfied with this answer and withdrew; but Zilu, who sat nearby, found it unacceptable and immediately spoke his mind: Leaving aside the issue of whether or not it was Benevolence, one had to admit that there was something splendid, transcending wisdom or the lack of it, in the act of trying to rectify one's country, completely ignoring all danger to oneself! Surely one could not dismiss this as a mere waste of one's life, despite the consequence.

"Zilu, you take note only of the splendid spirit to be found in such petty righteousness and seem unable to understand what is higher still. The gentlemen of ancient times would, if the Way were to be found in their state, devote themselves faithfully to its service; if the Way were not to be found in their state, they would withdraw and avoid service. You seem not yet to understand how splendid it is to advance or withdraw depending upon the state of things. It says in the Book of Poetry: 'When evil is rampant among the people, do not try to establish rules by yourself.' Now this seems to apply to Xieye's case."

"Well, then," began Zilu, after reflecting on this, "is keeping yourself safe the most important thing in this world? Not sacrificing yourself for the sake of righteousness? Is a man's judgment about whether he should advance or withdraw at a certain time more important than the well-being of the whole world? For if Xieye, disgusted at the corruption he saw before him, had withdrawn, it might have been good for himself; but what effect would it have had on the people of the state of Chen? If you consider the effect it would have on the spirit of the people, was it not, in fact, far more meaningful for him to have remonstrated with the ruler through his death, even though he knew it would bring no quick result?"

"I am by no means saying that one's personal safety is the only matter of importance," replied Confucius. "If I thought that, I would not have praised Bigan as a benevolent man. The point is that if one is to cast aside one's life for the sake of the Way, he must consider when and where to do so. To make that judgment with wisdom is not to act with an eye to personal benefit. To rush to die is not of itself a sign of high ability."

When it was put like that, one might agree; but something about it still did not sit well with Zilu. One could sense in the Master's words and actions a tendency to regard enlightened self-preservation as the highest wisdom at the same time that he insisted a man should sacrifice himself to accomplish Benevolence. This contradiction troubled Zilu. If the other disciples did not seem to be aware of the contradiction, it was because "enlightened self-preservation" was instinctive with them. Without that as their basis, the ideas of Benevolence and Righteousness would seem too dangerous to be borne.

When Zilu took his leave, seeming unconvinced, Confucius gazed after him and said with sorrow: "When a country has the Way, he is as straight as an arrow; likewise, when a country has not the Way, he is straight as an arrow. He is like Shiyu of Wei. He will not die a peaceful death, I fear."

When the state of Chu attacked the state of Wu, Shangyang, an official in charge of public works, was among those pursuing the Wu forces. He took up his bow after Prince Qi Ji, who was riding in the chariot with him, had declared, "By royal order, you may take bow in hand." Only after being further told "Now fire!" did he shoot an arrow, killing a man; at once he replaced his bow in its case. Again he was urged to shoot, so he took his bow out again and felled two more men. Each time his shot hit its mark, he covered his eyes. Having killed three men, he turned the chariot around and said, "I am of low rank and have now done enough to report on the success of my mission."

Confucius was filled with admiration at this account and exclaimed, "Even in killing, there is propriety to be observed!" To Zilu, however, this was ludicrous. In particular, Shangyang's thinking he had done his part by killing three men struck Zilu as a perfect example of an attitude he hated—valuing one's own actions above the welfare of the nation. It made his blood boil. Flushed with anger, he launched his argument at the Master: "The duty of a vassal serving his lord in a great matter is to exert all his strength and cease not until death! How can you approve of this man?" Confucius had no appropriate response. He simply laughed and said, "Yes, you are right. I was only admiring the man's unhappiness at having to take human life."

Thirteen

Zilu continued to follow Confucius, visiting Wei four times, spending three years in Chen, and traveling to Cao, Song, Cai, She, and Chu.

He had long before given up hope that any ruler would put the Master's Way into practice, yet, strangely enough, this apprehension no longer irritated him. After years of constant indignation at the muddled state of the world, the incapacity of the rulers, and the ill fortune of

Confucius, he had somehow arrived, in recent years, at an understanding of the destiny of Confucius and his followers. He was far from being passively resigned to their "fate"; or, if we are to use the word "fate," it was in a far more positive sense, involving realization of their mission as "a summons to all generations and all the world, not merely to a single small country or a single age." Now Zilu truly appreciated the meaning of the Master's proud statement when his group was besieged by a violent mob in the land of Kuang: "If Heaven does not yet wish to destroy my teachings, what can the men of Kuang do to me?" He realized how great was his teacher's wisdom in never giving in to despair, never arrogantly ignoring realities, and always doing his best within the given limitations. And now for the first time he understood the significance of Confucius' acting as if always aware of the regard of future generations. Perhaps because he was too intelligent, in a common way, the clever disciple Zigong had little awareness of this transcendental aspect of Confucius' mission. It was the candid and direct Zilu who was able to grasp the larger significance of the Master's work, perhaps because of his extremely pure and honest love of his teacher.

Year after year was spent wandering, until finally Zilu was fifty years of age. It would be false to suggest that he no longer had rough spots, but certainly he had become a solid, mature human being. His determination—as exemplified by his flashing eyes and his words "What would great wealth mean to me?"—was now far removed from the pointless bravado of a poor ronin and showed, rather, the worth and dignity of a man of real distinction.

Fourteen

Upon his fourth visit to Wei, Confucius, at the urging of the youthful duke of Wei and the high official Kong Shuyu, recommended Zilu for service to the state. When the Master, after more than ten years' of travel, returned to his native state, Zilu thus remained in Wei.

For these ten years, Wei had been mired in ceaseless strife, centering on Lady Nanzi's dissolute behavior. Gong Shuxu hatched a plot to get rid of Lady Nanzi, but then found himself slandered by her and forced into exile in Lu. Kuai Kui, the son of Duke Ling, who was the heir-apparent, tried to stab Lady Nanzi, his stepmother, but failed and fled to Jin. With the position of heir-apparent vacant, Duke Ling died. There was little choice but to designate Che, the young son of the absent Kuai Kui, as ruler, under the title Duke Chu. Kuai Kui, with support from Jin, infiltrated the western region of Wei, awaiting his chance to ascend the throne. As a result, Duke Chu was a son trying to prevent his father from taking power, while Kuai Kui was a father trying to seize the throne from his own son. Such was the state of affairs in the land of Wei, where Confucius had recommended that Zilu serve.

Zilu was appointed to govern the Pu region on behalf of the Kong family. The Kongs of Wei were a distinguished clan similar to the Ji Sun clan in Lu, and Kong Shuyu, the head of the family, was a talented official. Pu had been the fiefdom of Gong Shuxu, whom the present government had exiled due to the calumnies of Lady Nanzi, leaving the people of Pu angry and defiant on behalf of their former lord. They were a rather rough lot to begin with, Zilu himself having been attacked by a mob when he traveled there with Confucius some years before.

Before leaving on this assignment, Zilu sought Confucius' counsel about how to deal with Pu, of which it was said: "There are many ruffians in the villages, and they are hard to control." Confucius responded thus: "If you treat them with respect, even the brave can be made to obey. If you are broad-minded and just, the people will love you. If you are mild yet decisive, even the wicked can be suppressed." Zilu bowed in gratitude and set off on his assignment.

Zilu's first act in Pu was to summon the most powerful and the most rebellious men of the region. He did this not simply to tame and control them. Mindful that, as Confucius taught, "One cannot punish without first instructing," he wanted first to let them know his intentions. Zilu's unaffected frankness seemed to be well suited to the coarse local character, and they responded very positively. In fact, Zilu had been known throughout the empire as the most good-natured of Confucius' disciples. The Master's recommendation—"Only Zilu is capable of hearing one side in a dispute and justly deciding the case"—was widely spoken of, and greatly embellished in the telling. His reputation was doubtless one reason why the difficult men of Pu respected him so.

Three years later, Confucius happened to pass through Pu. Entering the fiefdom, he exclaimed: "How fine it is that Zilu is both respectful and faithful!" Then, moving through the village, he said: "How fine it is that Zilu is both loyal and magnanimous!" At last, upon stepping into Zilu's official mansion, he remarked: "How fine it is that Zilu is both insightful and decisive!" Zigong, who was holding the bit of the Master's horse, asked Confucius why he was praising Zilu before even seeing him. Confucius replied: "When I entered the fiefdom, I could see that the fields were well ordered, the wild grasses carefully cut back, and the irrigation ditches deeply dug. This is because the people, knowing their governor to be respectful and faithful, exert themselves to the utmost. When I passed through the village, I could see that the houses with their surrounding hedges were well kept and the trees were luxuriant. This is because the people, knowing their governor to be loyal and magnanimous, do not neglect their work. When at last I entered the courtyard of the official mansion, I could see that it was exceedingly clean and that there was not one servant who failed to obey orders. This is because, the words of the governor being insightful and decisive, the government is well conducted. Thus, I could learn everything about Zilu's mode of governing without yet meeting him."

Fifteen

Around the time that Duke Ai of Lu had gone hunting in Daye, in the western part of his domain, where he encountered a unicorn, Zilu arrived for a brief visit in Lu. Around the same time, Yeh, an official of the state of Xiao Zhu, betrayed his country and fled to Lu. Yeh had once met Zilu, and was duly impressed; thus he declared that if Zilu would act as his sponsor, he needed no further oath of protection from the state of Lu itself. (According to custom, an exile could be assured of sanctuary only if the host state provided a sworn guarantee; Yeh was willing to accept Zilu's sponsorship in lieu of that guarantee.) Such was

Zilu's reputation for honesty and fidelity that it was said of him: "He never puts off until tomorrow what he has once said he will do."

Zilu, however, flatly refused this request. Someone commented to Zilu: "The man says he would trust the word of you alone, rather than the sworn promise of a state of a thousand chariots. Nothing could honor a man more than to be trusted in this fashion. Why, then, are you ashamed to accept it?" Zilu replied: "If there should be conflict between Lu and Xiao Zhu, and if I were ordered to die fighting beneath Xiao Zhu's walls, I would gladly and unquestioningly obey. But this man Yeh is a disloyal minister who has betrayed his country. If I agreed to be his sponsor, I would be affirming his treason. How can you think I would do such a thing?"

Upon hearing this, those who knew Zilu well smiled; it was entirely in keeping with his character.

That same year, Chen Heng of Qi murdered his overlord. Confucius, who was serving as senior adviser to the government, fasted for three days and then went before Duke Ai and implored him to attack Qi for the sake of justice. Three times he asked, but the duke, fearing the military strength of Qi, would not give permission. Instead he suggested that Confucius appeal to Ji Sun for action, knowing that Ji Kangzi would never agree to this. Confucius explained to an acquaintance: "Being of official rank, however lowly, I could not but speak out." It was his duty to remonstrate, knowing well that it would do no good.

Zilu, hearing this, was saddened. Had the Master acted merely for form's sake, then? Was his response to injustice such that he could be content with no action? Even after nearly forty years of close association, the gap between Master and disciple could be unbridgeable.

Sixteen

While Zilu was away in Lu, Kong Shuyu, the most powerful political figure in Wei, died. His widow, Boji, was a cunning political strategist whose influence grew daily more prominent. Kong Kui had formally succeeded his father, but the real authority was Boji. Che, the reigning duke of Wei, was Boji's nephew, and the former heir-apparent who now sought the throne was her younger brother, Kuai Kui. She might have had warm ties with both, but a complex mix of affection and self-interest led her to favor inordinately her younger brother. Relying as her envoy on the handsome youth Hun Liangfu, a one-time court page whom she had come to favor exceedingly since the death of her husband, she was in frequent contact with Kuai Kui, quietly plotting to drive out the reigning young duke.

By the time Zilu returned to Wei, the struggle between father and son over the dukedom was intense, and the air was thick with political intrigue.

On a certain day in the twelfth intercalary month of the fortieth year in the reign of King Zhao, as evening drew near, a messenger from Luan Ning, the senior retainer of the Kong family, rushed frantically into the residence of Zilu. He bore this message: "Today, with the help of Boji and Liangfu, the former heir-apparent Kuai Kui secretly reentered the city! He is holding Kong Kui, demanding that he recognize Kuai Kui as Duke of Wei. The situation is dire. I am leaving for Lu, in the service of the present duke. I must leave the rest to you, sir."

"So it has come to this," thought Zilu. Feeling he could not remain silent after learning that Kong Kui, his immediate superior, was being held by force and subjected to threats, in haste he departed for the palace.

As he entered the outer gate, Zilu encountered a short, ugly fellow who was just leaving. It was Zigao, a younger disciple of Confucius, now an official of Wei upon Zilu's recommendation. This honest but timid man reported that the inner gate had been barred shut. "I do not care. We need to get in," said Zilu. "But it is already too late," exclaimed Zigao, "and we might find ourselves in terrible trouble." "We both serve the Kong family! Why should we be afraid of trouble?" replied Zilu harshly.

He shook off Zigao, and headed toward the inner gate. He pounded on it with his fists. "No entrance!" came a shout from within; it was a familiar voice. Zilu yelled: "Gong Sun-gan! It is I, Zilu. Open up! Do not change your colors. If you've taken someone's pay, you cannot abandon them when they need you. Open up!"

Just then the gate was opened to allow a messenger to leave, and Zilu slipped through. The courtyard was full of activity; retainers, who had been summoned to hear Kong Kui's supposed proclamation of support for a new duke, were in a dither, unsure of what position to take. On the balcony facing the courtyard, young Kong Kui stood uncomfortably, pressed between his stepmother Boji and his uncle Kuai Kui, preparing to announce the regime change.

From the back of the crowd, Zilu cried out: "This is wrong! This is an outrage! Even if you kill him, the side of Right will never be defeated!"

Zilu wanted first and foremost to save the youth he served. The crowd turned around to face him, and he tried to rouse them to action: "The heir-apparent is a coward and a fraud. If we set the balcony on fire, he will be so scared he will run. Set the balcony on fire, I say!" He pointed at the torches burning in the courtyard, and kept up his harangue: "Start a fire! Start a fire! All of us—we owe it to Kong Kui's father, so grab those torches and start a fire! Save Kong Kui! Save Kong Kui!"

Unnerved by this outburst, the usurper Kuai Kui ordered the swordsmen Shi Qi and Yu Yan to silence Zilu. Zilu had been a fighter in his youth, and he slashed back at them fearlessly with his sword. But the years had taken their toll on him, and gradually he found himself gasping for breath, defenseless. With the tide turning against Zilu, the retainers revealed their true colors: they jeered and hurled sticks and stones at him. The point of a spear now grazed his cheek, severing the cord of his cap of office. Zilu clutched his cap, trying to hold it in place, and then felt a sword slice into his shoulder. Blood spurted out, and he fell to the ground, his cap slipping from his head. He grabbed it and put it back on his head, quickly tying the cord that had been cut. He was drenched in blood. Summoning a last burst of energy, he bellowed: "All of you, look! This is how a gentleman dies—with his cap of office in place!"

And so Zilu died, his body cut and chopped like mincemeat for the table.

When Confucius had first heard about the political upheavals in Wei, he stated: "Zigao will return to Lu, but Zilu will die in Wei." Learning that his prophecy had been correct, the old sage stood for a time with his eyes closed in prayer, and then silently wept. Upon hearing that Zilu's corpse had been preserved in salt, like that of a common criminal, he ordered that all salted foods in his household be thrown out; thereafter, salted mincemeats were never allowed at his table.

Translated by Paul McCarthy

The Rebirth of Wujing

I t was early autumn, as forlorn cicadas cried in the withering willows and the Antares in Scorpio inclined toward the west. The monk Tripitaka, accompanied by two disciples, anxiously hurried over arduous terrain. Suddenly they came upon a river so wide they could not see the far shore. There were great roiling waves. Climbing the embankment to survey the area, they discovered a stone monument inscribed with the ideographs "Liu Sha He," the River of Flowing Sand, in official seal–style characters. Below were four lines of verse:

> *Eight hundred li wide, the River of Flowing Sand;*
> *Three thousand fathoms deep, the water of the Mystical Realm—*
> *Even goose down will not float*
> *And a reed flower will surely sink.*
> — *Journey to the West*

One

Of the thirteen thousand monsters and goblins inhabiting the

River of Flowing Sand, none was as unsure of himself as Wujing. As punishment for eating nine monks, the skulls of the monks were attached permanently to his neck. These skulls, however, were visible only to himself. None of the other monsters could see them. "They are all in your mind," they said. Wujing would look dubiously at them, and then he would look down, as if to say, "Why am I so different from others?" The other monsters said to one another: "He has barely eaten ordinary human beings, let alone monks. Nobody has seen him do this. All we have seen him eat is crucian carp and small fry." They nicknamed him Talk-to-Himself Wujing. He was constantly beset by uneasiness and regret, and as a result, the pitiful self-accusations in his mind often spilled out in talk to himself. From a distance it might appear that tiny bubbles were coming out of his mouth, when in fact they were mutterings on the order of the following: "I am a fool." "Why am I like this?" "I am a failed celestial being." "I can see my doom."

At this time, it was commonly believed that not only monsters but also all living beings were reincarnations. Everyone in the riverbed talked of how Wujing had once been the captain of the Royal Screens of State at the Palace of Divine Clouds in the celestial realm. Finally, even the extremely skeptical Wujing himself had to pretend that he believed it. But the truth was, he—and he was alone in this as well—harbored doubts about reincarnation:

Supposing the captain of the Royal Screens five hundred years ago has become this "I" of the present—well, can we say that the captain of the Royal Screens of long ago is the same as this "I" of the present? I do not remember a single thing about the celestial realm of those days. How can the captain of the Royal Screens of a time before I can remember and this present self of mine be the same? Is it the physical body that is the same? Or is it the soul? By the way, what exactly is the soul?

When Wujing voiced these kinds of questions, his fellow monsters would laugh: "There he goes again." There would be some who mocked him, but there would be others who showed pity. "He is sick," they said. "His condition is due to a terrible sickness."

In fact, Wujing was sick.

When and by what course he had become sick, Wujing did not know. It was simply—when he became aware of it—a hateful thing thickly enveloping him. He disliked doing anything; everything he saw depressed him; he hated himself with regards to everything; he could not trust himself. For days on end, he hid in a cave, ate nothing, and, with eyes glaring, sank deep in thought. He would suddenly rouse himself, walk around, mutter to himself, and just as suddenly sit down. He was unaware of the gestures he made. The source of his uneasiness— that was unknown to him as well. Everything that he had accepted as a matter of course began to appear incomprehensible and doubtful. What had seemed to be a single unified whole now appeared disparate and unconnected, and, while he thought about the parts, he could no longer divine the whole.

An aged fish monster, who was a doctor, astrologer, and shaman, said this to him: "Oh, I feel great sorrow for you. You have contracted an unfortunate sickness. Ninety-nine out of a hundred people who get this disease live in misery for the rest of their lives. This illness did not originally exist among us, but after we began to eat human beings, there came to be instances, though rare, of affliction. A being who has been afflicted loses his ability to accept matters uncritically. Regardless of what he sees or whom he meets, he immediately wonders, 'Why?' He focuses on the genuine, ultimate 'why?'—the answer to which God alone knows. To focus on this question gets in the way of living life. In our world it is agreed that living beings should not think of such matters, is it not? The most troubling consequence of this condition is the doubts about one's own 'self' that the illness causes a being to harbor. Why do I think of me as me? Would it cause problems if I thought of someone else as me? What exactly is 'I'? To start thinking in this fashion is the worst symptom of this disease. That is your condition, is it not? Alas, for this sickness there is no medicine, no doctor. The patient must heal himself. Unless you are blessed with special opportunity, there will not be a time when your face will be free of the cloud that darkens it."

Two

The invention of writing had been introduced into their world from the human world long before this time. But while writing was common, it was customary for river beings to scorn it. The belief, widely held, was that living wisdom could not possibly be conferred through such a dead medium as writing. (Drawing a picture, on the other hand, offered a better chance of capturing it.) It would be as foolish as trying to catch smoke in one's hand while keeping its shape intact. Therefore, contrary to what one might conventionally think, the ability to read was rejected by monsters as a sign of diminished life energy. It was thought among them that Wujing's chronic melancholy owed to the fact that he could read.

Although writing was held in low esteem, thinking was not looked down upon. Among the thirteen thousand monsters, quite a few were philosophers. Because their vocabulary was extremely limited, however, even the most complex issues were considered in the simplest words. Each philosopher monster had a "thinking shop" at the bottom of the River of Flowing Sand, and a kind of philosophical melancholy thus hovered above the riverbed.

A certain wise, old fish had purchased a house with a beautiful garden, and under a sunny window, he meditated on the notion of eternal happiness without regret. A certain noble school of fish, in the shade of bright green algae, strummed their harps as they praised the musical harmony of the universe. The ugly, slow, foolishly honest Wujing, who did not try to hide his silly suffering, was fair game for these intellectual monsters. One monster asked Wujing with a solemn air, "What is truth?" But he did not wait for a reply, and walked away with large strides and a derisive smile. Another monster, the spirit of a blowfish, having heard about Wujing's sickness, took the time to visit him. He had assumed that Wujing suffered from "fear of death," and he came to laugh at him. "While we have life, we have no death. When death arrives, already the self does not exist. Why should we fear death at all?" the blowfish monster said. Wujing promptly acknowledged the correctness of this argument. That was because Wujing was not afraid of death. The cause of his sickness did not originate from any fear. The blowfish spirit left disappointed.

In the world of monsters, body and mind were not clearly separated as in the human world; so Wujing's sickness of the mind had the immediate result of severe physical torture and suffering. Unable to endure the pain, he made up his mind:

Now that things have reached this point, no matter how much trouble it may be, and no matter how much I am ridiculed, I will personally visit all the wise men, doctors, and astrologers on the bottom of this river, and seek their wisdom.

He put on a plain monk's habit and set off.

Why were monsters "monsters" and not human beings? It was because they had focused on one attribute of their being to a degree so extreme that it grew out of balance with other attributes and they had become deformed, ugly, and nonhuman. Some monsters were gluttons; therefore, their mouths and stomachs were inordinately large. Others were lascivious, and so their genitalia had developed obscenely. There were others who prided themselves on intellectual purity, to the point that, aside from their heads, their bodies had atrophied. They were obsessed with the absoluteness of their worldview and had no interest in the thoughts of others. That is why, at the bottom of the River of Flowing Sand, hundreds of metaphysical systems swayed, like countless water plants, separately, never in harmony with others—some with the calm joy of despair, some with boundless cheer, some with wishful, hopeless sighs.

Three

Wujing first called upon Hei Luan, a famous Taoist master of magic. Hei Luan had built his abode by piling up rocks on the bottom of a fairly shallow part of the river. At its entrance was calligraphy that read "Cave of the Slanting Moon and Three Stars." The master had the face of a fish and the body of a human being; rumor had it that he was able to appear and disappear at will, create thunder in winter, make ice in summer, cause birds to run and beasts to fly.

Wujing served this master for three months. He did not care about magic tricks, but he reasoned that, if the master was skilled in magic, then he was probably a Taoist sage, and a sage would have comprehended the Way of the universe and possessed the wisdom to cure his illness. But Wujing was disappointed. Whether it was the Taoist master seated on a huge turtle at the innermost part of the cave, or the several dozen disciples surrounding him, all the talk was about the miraculous, wonderful art of magic. They also spoke practically—of how, with the use of magic, to deceive enemies or obtain treasure. No one had interest in the "useless" thinking Wujing sought. In the end, ridiculed and laughed at, Wujing was driven out of the Cave of the Slanting Moon and Three Stars.

Wujing next visited the residence of Sha Hong, the spirit of the aged prawn who lived as a hermit. His back was bent like a bow, and he lived half-buried in the sand. For three months Wujing served this old hermit and, while providing personal care to him, Wujing gained exposure to the depth of his philosophy. As Wujing rubbed his back, the hermit, with a serious expression, said the following: "The world is empty. Is there a single thing in this world that is good? If there is, that would only be the fact that the end of this world will come someday. There is no need for complex reasoning. Look around us—incessant changes, anxiety, anguish, fear, disillusionment, strife, boredom. Truly, we are in an unenlightened, obscure, and confused state, with no destination in sight. We are alive only at the present moment. Moreover, the present moment immediately disappears into the past from under our feet. The next moment and the moment after that are exactly the same, like the sand beneath the feet of a traveler standing on a crumbling dune. Where can we rest safely? Because we will fall if we stop, we have no choice but to continue running down the slope—that is our life. Happiness? An imaginary concept; it never refers to a specific real condition. It is just a fragile hope that has gained a name."

Seeing Wujing's anxious face, the hermit added these words, as if to console him: "But, young man, you need not fear so much. Those who are swept away by the waves will drown, but those who ride the waves will go over them. It is not impossible to ride over these ups and downs of life and to arrive at a state of indestructibility and immobility. Sages of long ago were able to transcend right and wrong, transcend good and evil, forget the self, forget things, and arrive at the realm of no-death-no-life. But, as has been said since ancient times, it would be a great mistake to think that such a state is enjoyable. There is no pain, but neither is there the pleasure that ordinary creatures have. Tasteless and colorless. Indeed, it is quite insipid, like wax or sand."

Wujing spoke modestly: "What I wish to ask of is not such matters as individual happiness or firmness of mind, but the ultimate meaning of the self and of the world."

The hermit blinked his mucus-filled eyes and replied: "The self? The world? Do you think that outside of the self an objective world exists? What we call the world is an illusion that the self projects between time and space. When the self dies, the world disappears. To think that the world remains after the self dies is vulgar and mistaken. Even if the world disappears, this unknowable self will continue without change."

In the morning of exactly the ninetieth day of Wujing's visit, following several days of severe abdominal pain and diarrhea, the old hermit died. He was rejoicing in the prospect that by his death he would obliterate the objective world that had given him such agonizing abdominal pain and ugly diarrhea.

Wujing carefully performed the funeral rites for Sha Hong, and with tears in his eyes he again embarked on his journey.

According to rumor, Zuo Wang always sat in Zen meditation, asleep; he awoke every fiftieth day. He believed that the world of dreams was reality, and on the rare occasions when he was awake, he believed it was a dream. Wujing traveled a great distance to visit this master, and when he arrived, as expected, the master was asleep. Since the cave was at the bottom of the deepest valley in the River of Flowing Sand, where light from above barely penetrated, it was difficult for Wujing to see clearly. Eventually, as his eyes adjusted to the dark, before him appeared a vague figure of a monk seated in the lotus position, sleeping. Where Wujing now stood, no sounds from the outside could be heard; rarely did fish swim by. So, having little choice, Wujing sat before Zuo Wang, the Master Sit-in-Abstraction, and tried closing his eyes; it was so quiet he felt as if his hearing was failing.

Four days later, the master opened his eyes. He seemed neither to see nor not to see Wujing, who hurriedly rose to his feet and bowed before him. The master merely blinked. After they had faced each other silently, Wujing spoke timidly: "Master, I am sorry to bother you, but I have a question. What exactly is 'I'?"

"Tut! Useless giant crane Dalizuan of ancient Qin!" the master scolded, at the same time striking Wujing on the head with a Zen stick. Wujing was stunned, but reseated himself correctly and, after a while, uttered the same question. This time no stick came down upon him.

Master Sit-in-Abstraction parted his thick lips, moving no other part of his body, and now answered in words as from a dream: "The one who feels hunger when he gets no food for a long time is you. The one who feels the chill when winter comes is you." With that, he sealed his lips and looked in the direction of Wujing; slowly he closed his eyes.

Wujing waited patiently. On the fiftieth day, Master Sit-in-Abstraction awoke, and seeing Wujing sitting in front of him, he mumbled, "Are you still here?" Wujing replied humbly that he had been waiting for fifty days. "Fifty days?" said the master, turning his dreamy, sleepy eyes on Wujing, and sat silent and still for a few hours. Then he spoke:

"Those who do not know that the measure of time is nothing other than the actual feeling of the person who feels it are fools. They say that in the human world the mechanism to measure the length of time has been made, but it will probably sow the seed of great misunderstanding. The long life of the legendary great camellia tree and the short life of a single-day mushroom are no different in length. Time is a mechanism in our mind."

The master closed his eyes again. Wujing, who knew that those eyes would not open again for fifty days, respectfully bowed to the sleeping master and left.

"Fear! Tremble! And believe in God!" shouted a young man standing at the busiest crossroads in the River of Flowing Sand.

"Think how our short life is submerged in the endless eternity before and after it. Think how the small space we live in is thrown into the limitless expanse which we do not know and which does not know us! Who can escape trembling with terror at the smallness and insignificance of our own figure? We are all prisoners on death row, chained by iron shackles. Each moment a number from among us are killed right before our eyes. We have no hope of reprieve, and simply await our turn. The time is drawing near. Are you trying to pass that brief time in self-deception and intoxication? You cursed cowards! In that interval, do you intend to remain smugly self-satisfied, relying on your miserable rationality? You arrogant fools do not know your place! You cannot control even a single sneeze with your impoverished will, can you?"

The cheeks of the fair-complexioned youth were flushed, and he did not stop his harangue until he was hoarse. Where in this noble, graceful figure did that fierceness reside? Wujing gazed at the youth's beautiful, burning eyes, amazed. He had felt the fiery, holy arrows of the youth's words come shooting toward his soul.

"All we can do is love God and hate ourselves. A part is not the main component; it is conceit to imagine the part as independent. We must, to the end, take the will of the whole as our own will, and live our lives for the benefit of the whole. Those who become one with God will become one in spirit."

Certainly this was the voice of a superior soul, thought Wujing. Yet, within himself, he understood this was not the wisdom he sought. Teaching was like medicine, and giving medication for a tumor to a patient with malaria would not cure his illness.

Not far from the crossroads, Wujing encountered a beggar crouching by the roadside. He was a hunchback who was terribly disfigured.

Because his backbone arched so high, his head hung lower than his shoulders, his jaw almost touching his navel. His back was covered with festering boils. Wujing let a sigh escape. The beggar, who could not move his head freely, turned his bloodshot eyes upward to glare at Wujing, and sneered, revealing a single remaining long front tooth. Then, dangling the arms that were hinged up high, he staggered over to Wujing, looked up at him, and said, "It's presumptuous of you to pity me, young man. Do you think that I deserve your pity? Perhaps you are the more to be pitied. You think I feel bitterness toward the Creator for this body I inhabit? I do not. On the contrary, I praise the Creator for my unusual form! I look forward to what further shape my body will take henceforth! If my left elbow becomes a rooster, I will make it crow to tell time. If my right elbow becomes a slingshot, I will fell an owl to roast for a meal. If my buttocks become wheels and my soul becomes a horse, I will have the finest, most convenient carriage. How about it? Are you surprised? My name is Ziyu, and I have three good friends, Zisi, Zili, and Zilai. We are disciples of Master Nujushi, and we have transcended the form of beings and entered the realm of no-life-no-death. In water we do not get wet, in fire we do not burn; we do not dream when asleep, and we do not worry when awake. Just the other day, the four of us were saying: 'We take nothingness as our head, life as our back, and death as our bottom.' Ha, ha, ha, ha . . ."

Wujing was startled. He wondered if this beggar was not in fact a Taoist sage. If his words were genuine, then they were truly admirable. The beggar's words and his attitude, however, bore a hint of exaggeration, and this led Wujing to suspect that the beggar was forcing himself to speak bravely while enduring great pain; also, it may be said that the ugliness of the man and the stench of his pus repelled Wujing. He was attracted to the beggar, but he decided against serving him. Yet he wished to seek instruction from Master Nujushi, whom the beggar had mentioned, so he told the beggar this.

"Oh, you ask about my master! The master has his hermitage ten thousand eight hundred leagues to the north, where the River of Flowing Sand meets the Red River and the Black River. If your desire to seek the Way is firm, he would be an excellent teacher. I encourage you to make all effort to pursue your goal. Also, please give the master my best regards," said the hunchback haughtily, squaring his pointy shoulders with all his might.

Four

Wujing traveled north toward the junction of the River of Flowing Sand with the Black River and the Red River. At night he slept among the reeds, and when morning came, again he walked north over the endless sand plains of the riverbed. Whenever he encountered schools of fish swimming about, joyously flashing their silver scales, he would ponder why he alone did not feel joy in his heart. Every day he walked. He made it a rule to knock at the gates of all the notable Taoists and ascetics on his path.

When he visited Master Qiuran Nianzi, the dragon-whiskered catfish monster, who was well known for his greed and physical strength, had this to say as he stroked his whiskers: "If one considers only the remote future, there will be worries about the present. The being who understands life will not take too broad a view of life."

"Take, for example, this fish," he said, snatching a carp swimming by and immediately munching on it. "It would be appropriate for philosophers and immortals to consider why this fish was fated to pass before my eyes and become my meal; however, if I were engaged in such long drawn-out thoughts, my meal would escape. First catch the carp, bite it, and then think about the question. It would not be too late. Why is a carp a carp? How does a carp differ metaphysically from a crucian carp? And so on and so forth. To be entangled in these foolish, elevated questions and miss catching the carp—that is the type of being you are, are you not? The melancholy light in your eyes tells me so. Am I not right?"

Wujing hung his head, thinking that certainly was the case. The catfish monster, who had by this time consumed the carp, was focusing, his eyes glinting, on Wujing's lowered neck. Suddenly Wujing heard the sound of saliva being swallowed and stepped back reflexively—just as the razor-sharp nails of the catfish monster came flying at his throat. He escaped with only scrapes. The monster, furious at failing to land the first blow, came charging at Wujing. Wujing kicked strongly, which caused a cloud of sediment to rise, and in a panic he fled from the cave. "I now understand the harsh principle of real life," Wujing thought, trembling.

Wujing next attended a lecture by a priest in the spirit of a crab named Wu Chang Gongzi, also known as Lord No Bowels-No Mercy, who was preaching the gospel of neighborly love. In the middle of the lecture, the priest was so overcome by hunger that, in plain sight of all assembled, he ate several of his own children. Of course, because he was a crab, he hatched countless children at a time, but still Wujing was astounded.

When the priest finished his snack, he continued with his message of mercy and forbearance without missing a beat. Had the priest forgotten the fact that he had just eaten his children to satisfy his hunger? Perhaps the fact had not even registered in his consciousness. Perhaps that is the lesson that I should learn, Wujing thought. Where in my life have I committed such an instinctual, unselfconscious act? He knelt and bowed. No, he thought further, my flaw is that I find it necessary to attach a conceptual understanding to all experience. I must absorb lessons in their raw form, without packing them into canned goods. Yes, that is right, that is so. Wujing bowed once again and respectfully departed.

The hermitage of Puyizi, Master Reed Garment, was an unusual dwelling of practitioners of the Way. There were several disciples, each emulating the master in seeking to unlock the mysteries of nature. But rather than seekers, they might be better described as enraptured beings. Their practice was simply to observe nature and be filled by its beauty and harmony.

"First, we must learn to feel," said one disciple. "We must refine our senses in the most beautiful and wise way possible. Thoughts separated from the direct perception of natural beauty are gray dreams. As you look at nature, make your heart look deeply inward. Clouds, sky, wind, snow, pale blue ice, swaying red seaweed, lights of algae glittering in the water at night, the chambered spiral of the nautilus, the crystals of amethyst, the red of garnet, the blue of fluorite—how beautifully these things tell the secrets of nature." His words were like a poet's.

"And yet," continued a second disciple, "a step away from understanding nature's secrets, suddenly the happy premonition vanishes, and we must once again view the profile of a beautiful but cold nature. This is because our senses have not been sufficiently trained, our minds have not delved deeply enough. We must devote ourselves to greater effort, until ultimately, we experience moments when, as our master teaches, 'To observe is to love, and to love is to create.'"

Throughout this conversation, the master himself said not a word. He was gazing at a piece of brilliant green malachite in the palm of his hand, a calm and joyous expression in his eyes.

Wujing stayed a month at this hermitage. He, too, became nature's poet, praising the harmony of the universe and seeking with his innermost being to become one with nature.

While he acknowledged that this was not the right place for him, he was drawn to the quiet happiness of the group.

One of the disciples was an extraordinarily beautiful boy. His skin was translucent, like that of ice fish; the pupils of his eyes were large, as if he were dreaming; and the curls over his forehead fell softly, like the down of a dove's breast. When he was the least bit melancholy, a faint shadow crossed his exquisite face, like thin clouds passing before the moon; and when he felt joy, the depth of his calm, clear eyes shone like jewels in the night. Often he could be found dripping pale honey on top of white stones, outlining an image of the morning glory. His fellow disciples loved him, as did the master. He was gentle and pure, and his mind knew no doubt. If anything, he was too beautiful, too delicate, as if he were formed from a rarefied ether; this sensitivity left others feeling a vague uneasiness.

One morning, the boy left the grounds of the hermitage and never returned. He had gone out with another disciple, who brought back this report: the disciple happened to look away, and when he turned back he witnessed the beautiful boy melting into water. The other disciples found this absurd and laughed, but Master Reed Garment stopped them: the boy had such purity, he said, that indeed such a thing was possible.

Wujing, hearing this, could not but compare the robustness of the catfish monster, who had tried to make a meal of him, with the delicate beauty of the boy, who had melted into the water. And with these thoughts, he took leave of Master Reed Garment several days later.

Wujing next visited Banyi Guipo. Old Madam Perch in Mottled Attire was a female monster over five hundred years of age, yet her skin was as supple as a virgin's and her seductive figure capable of reducing hearts of iron and stone into things of putty. Her only credo in life was to taste the utmost pleasures of the flesh, and to this end she kept a stable of attractive young men in several dozen chambers in her inner courtyard. When she indulged in her pleasures, she would sever all association with the outside world, seeing neither relatives nor friends. Secreted in her inner quarters, she satisfied her desires day and night, and would only come up for air every third month.

Wujing chanced to arrive just as she was emerging from her inner quarters. Upon learning that Wujing was a seeker of the Way, Old Madam Perch had this to say, even as she showed hints of languorous fatigue in her attractive figure:

"This is the Way. The teachings of holy and wise men and the ascetic practices of immortals and philosophers all aim to maintain such a moment of supreme ecstasy. To have breath in this world is a precious gift, even in the limitlessness of time and kalpas that number like the grains of sand along the Ganges. On the other hand, death comes in a hurry. What else is there for us, for whom life is dear and death so easy, than to think about this other Way? Oh, such exciting delight, that intoxication always new!" exclaimed the female monster, narrowing her alluring eyes.

"Because you are, alas, ugly, I will not ask you to stay. So I will speak the truth: Each year a hundred young men in my inner courtyard die from exhaustion. They each of them die happily, satisfied with their life. Not a single young man has died regretting his having resided here. There have been some, however, who regretted dying because they could no longer enjoy such pleasure."

Pitying Wujing for his ugliness, Old Madam Perch added this:

"What is 'virtue' but the ability to enjoy."

Grateful that because of his ugliness he did not have to join the ranks of the hundred men who die each year in the arms of Old Madam Perch, Wujing continued on his journey.

He posed the question "What is the self?" to each sage he encountered. The ideas of the sages, he found each time, were so different and so varied one from the other that Wujing did not know whom to believe.

One sage responded to the question with this: "Try uttering a cry. If you 'oink,' then you are a pig. If you 'honk,' then you are a goose."

Another sage preached: "If you do not force yourself to describe the self, then it is relatively less difficult to know the self."

Still another said this: "The eye can see everything, but it cannot see itself. The self is what the self cannot know."

And another sage said this: "The self is always the self. The self has called itself the self throughout the infinity before the birth of the present consciousness of self. No one remembers it now, however. In short, that self became the present self. Throughout the infinity after the present consciousness of self has perished, there will again be the self.... That self no one can now foresee, and when the time comes, it will have completely forgotten about the present consciousness of self."

Finally there was a sage who proclaimed: "What is one continuous self? It is the accumulation of the shadow of memory." This sage went on: "Losing memory is all that we do each day. Because we have forgotten the fact that we have forgotten an event, various events feel new to us; but in truth, it is because we have forgotten everything completely that anything seems new. Not only events from yesterday, but also events from a moment ago. In other words, the sense of perception and the emotion of that moment—in the next moment we will have forgotten all. Merely the blurred replicas of a very small part of them remain. That is why I can say, Wujing, how wonderful the present moment is!"

In five years of wandering, Wujing had repeated the foolish act of asking each sage he met the same question; the result he got was not unlike a sick person seeking a cure from physician after physician after physician—each treatment prescribed was different. In the end, Wujing found that he had become no wiser. Instead, he felt he had become light and insubstantial, as if he were not materially himself, incomprehensible. As for his old self, even though he had been ignorant, at least he had been physically solid, at least his body had had its own weight. But now, he had no weight at all, he could be blown away by a puff of air. He was attired in various patterns on the outside, but on the inside he was hollow. This is not good, thought Wujing. Surely, in his search for meaning there had to be a more direct path than all this thinking. How silly he had been to seek answers as if there were a calculus to the question. With this realization, Wujing walked on, stepping into water that was a murky reddish-black, and then he arrived at his next destination, the abode of Master Nujushi.

At first glance, Master Nujushi, whom Zhuangzi first introduced, had the appearance of an extremely ordinary Taoist immortal; he could even have been taken for a naïve simpleton. Wujing had come to serve and learn from him, but the master demurred. It seemed that, as the Taoist principle taught, "Being hard and strong is being dead, and being soft and weak is being alive," the master eschewed the intensity of desiring "to learn, to learn." On rare occasions, and to no one in particular, he was observed to be muttering. At such times, Wujing would prick up his ears, but the master's voice was so soft that Wujing could not discern what he was saying.

For three months, the only words Wujing had heard from the master were: "What a foolish man knows about himself is more than what an intelligent man can know about someone else; therefore, one must cure one's own sickness." Prepared to give up and move on, Wujing approached the Master to announce his departure. At this point Master Nujushi had several things he was willing to say: on the "foolishness of grieving over the fact that one does not have three eyes"; on the "unhappiness of a person who is not satisfied unless he can control by his will even the growth of his nails or hair"; on the need "for one not to denigrate thinking in its entirety . . . the happiness of a person who does not think is similar to pigs that do not get seasick . . . it is thinking about thinking that should be avoided."

Master Nujushi did not stop; he talked further about a demon who possessed godlike knowledge. There was nothing the demon did not know, from matters on a grand scale such as the movement of the stars, to matters on a minute scale such as the life cycle of microorganisms. He was able to use subtle, erudite calculations to go back in time and understand all the events that had taken place, and also to be able to predict future events. The demon, however, was very unhappy. This was because when he encountered the question why—not the how of the process but the fundamental why—all the events of the world occurred in the way they did, he had no answer. He could comprehend the fact of their existence, but his erudite, subtle calculations could not give him a reason. Why are sunflowers yellow? Why is grass green? Why is anything the way it is? This question tormented and troubled this demon of vast supernatural powers, ultimately leading him to a miserable death.

Master Nujushi talked about a very small, shabby demon, a sprite who said he was born to search for a certain small, gleaming object. No one knew what that gleaming object was, but the sprite searched for it constantly, and he lived for that purpose and died for that purpose. No small, gleaming object was ever found, but the life of this small, shabby demon was an extremely happy one.

As the master told these stories, he explained nothing of their meaning to Wujing. Only in the end did the master make the following admonitions:

"Blessed is he who knows sacred madness. For he will save himself by killing himself. The one who does not know sacred madness is cursed, for he will perish by neither killing himself nor making himself live. To love is a nobler way of understanding, and to live is a clearer way of thinking. Poor Wujing, he cannot help but soak everything in the poisonous juice of consciousness! The great changes that determine our fate occur without the involvement of consciousness. Think of this: when you were born, were you aware of it?"

Humbly Wujing responded: "Especially now, the teachings of the master have been made clear and comprehensible personally. During my many years of wandering, I, too, began to see that thinking alone was pulling me deeper and deeper into a muddy quagmire. However,

I cannot break through my present self and be reborn, and that is why I suffer."

Master Nujushi replied: "When the mountain stream flows to the precipice, it swirls around once, and then falls in a cascade. Wujing, you are now one step before that whirlpool, and you are hesitating. Once you take that step and are pulled into the whirlpool, you are only a breath away from hell. There is no time to think, reflect, or hesitate along the way. Timid Wujing! You look with dread and pity upon those who are swirling in the eddy, ready to fall, while you hesitate whether or not you yourself will take the plunge. You know full well that sooner or later you, too, must fall to the bottom of the valley. You also know that, even though you may choose not to be pulled into the whirlpool, it does not bring you happiness. After all that, do you still feel rooted in the position of bystander, unable to leave it? Those who are gasping in the terrible maelstrom of life are, contrary to what one may expect, not as unhappy as they might appear; they are, at the least, many times happier than the skeptical bystander. Ignorant Wujing—do you not know that?"

Wujing felt the value of the master's teachings down to the marrow of his bones. Yet as he took leave of the master, a part of him remained unsatisfied.

He decided that he would no longer seek instruction in the Way. "Each and every sage might seem important, but in truth they know nothing at all," he said to himself. Setting out on his journey home, he had this understanding: "Everyone lives with the premise, 'Let us pretend that we know, because all of us know as plain as day that we do not know.' If such a premise exists, then what a dull-witted trouble-maker am I, who makes such a big commotion, crying, 'I do not know, I do not know.'"

Five

Because Wujing was slow and dull-witted, he could not perform brilliant acts, such as achieving sudden enlightenment or experiencing a great revelation of truth. Nevertheless, gradually, unseen changes seemed to work on him.

He saw his situation as similar to placing a bet. When we are allowed to choose between two paths—one, which is eternal mud, and the other, which has a possibility of salvation despite the roughness of the way—then obviously everyone would choose the latter. Then why was he hesitating? At that point, for the first time, Wujing became aware of a base calculation in his thinking. If he chose the difficult path and suffered for it and ended up not being saved after all, then it would be an irredeemable loss; it was this calculation that had affected him unconsciously and resulted in his indecision. To avoid a waste of effort, he had remained on the smoother path that required less struggle but that would lead inevitably to decisive loss. That was the consequence of his lazy, stupid, base way of thinking.

While Wujing was staying at the abode of Master Nujushi, his feelings had been channeled in a single direction, into a corner. From there they began gradually to alter course so that they sprang from a degree of spontaneity. Until then, Wujing had thought he was seeking the meaning of the world, not his own happiness. This was, however, an utter misconception. The truth was that he was, in an unusual manner, most tenaciously seeking his own happiness. Wujing now began to understand this. He accepted, without self-deprecation, with a sense of peace, that he was not so grand a creature as to be able to contemplate the meaning of the world. He also began to summon the courage, before miring himself in overarching questions, to develop something of himself he had not known before: "Before I hesitate, I should try. Without thinking about success or failure, I will try, for the sake of trying, my utmost. It does not matter if it ends in failure." He who had always demurred from life for fear of failure no longer disliked wasted effort.

Six

Wujing was utterly exhausted.

He collapsed one day by the side of the road and fell into a deep slumber. It was a coma-like sleep, in which he forgot everything. He remained in this deep slumber for several days. He forgot hunger, and he did not dream.

When he awoke, he found himself immersed in a pale light. It was night, and the light of a full spring moon was diffused by the water of the shallow riverbed where he lay. Refreshed after a sound sleep, Wujing got up. He was hungry. As fish swam by, he reached out and caught them, and they became his meal. He then quaffed the saké from the gourd tied to his waist. It was delicious, and he drank it all in one continuous swallow, his throat making glugging sounds. His spirits high, he decided to take a walk.

The moonlight was so bright that each grain of sand seemed to be illuminated. On the plants swaying in the current, tiny bubbles gleamed like drops of mercury. Little fish now darted away at the sight of him, their white bellies flashing as they disappeared behind green algae. Wujing felt tipsy. He felt like singing. He was about to burst into song when suddenly he heard from the distance a song being sung. He stopped in his path to listen. At times the singing seemed to come from somewhere out of the river, at times from somewhere deep inside it. This was the song:

> In the land south of the Yangzi,
> The spring breeze has yet to blow.
> A partridge sings in the blossoming tree.
> Riding above three-tiered waves,
> A fish transforms into a dragon.
> Foolish men still dip for water
> From the fishless pond at night.

Wujing sat. In this world of the river in the blue-white moonlight, the singing carried like the sound of a horn in the wind.

He was not asleep; yet he was not awake. He stayed where he sat, almost in a trance. A gently throbbing pain seemed to permeate his soul, and now he entered into a world that might have been a dream or a vision. Water plants and fish vanished from his field of vision, and an indescribable fragrance of orchid and musk wafted by. Two unfamiliar figures approached him.

The first was a sturdy, formidable man holding a priest's staff. Behind him was an individual who looked like no ordinary human being. He was wearing a jeweled crown and necklace, and his face had a singular splendor, as solemn as it was serene. He appeared to be a Buddhist deity, with an *ushnisha*, the raised mound of flesh on the top of his head, and a faint halo. As the two drew near, the first man spoke: "I am Moksha Huian, the second prince of the Pagoda-Carrying Heavenly King. And this is my master, the Holy Father, the Great Bodhisattva Guanyin of the Southern Sea. My Holy Father bestows his compassion equally upon the eight protectors of Buddhism—the *devas*, the *naga* dragon-kings, the *yaksha* demons, the music-playing *gandharvas*, the angry *asura* demons, the heavenly golden *garuda* birds, the heavenly musician *kimnaras*, and the snake-headed *mahoraga* gods—as well as upon human and nonhuman beings. My master saw your suffering, Wujing, and he has made this sojourn to grace you with ordination into the Buddhist priesthood. Listen with gratitude."

Wujing found himself lowering his head, and to his ears now came the most beautiful music, the most exquisitely gentle and soft voice, the harmonic strains of the tide, signifying the ever-recurring benevolence of the Buddha.

"Wujing, ponder my words well. Oh, presumptuous Wujing! To say that one has gained knowledge when one has not, or to say that one has proven what one has not—the Lord Buddha criticizes this as arrogance. Therefore, someone like you, who sought to prove what could not be proven, cannot be called anything else but extremely arrogant. What you seek is something that even arhats and self-enlightened Buddhas have not yet been able to obtain; indeed they would not try to obtain. Poor Wujing! How did your wretched soul enter such a labyrinth? If you attain the correct way of thinking and perceiving, the pure deeds necessary for salvation can be accomplished immediately. However, the state of your mind-heart is weakened and has fallen into an ill-conceived way of thinking and perceiving. As a result, you now encounter the infinite suffering of the Three Evil Paths.

"Since you cannot be saved by meditation, abandon henceforth all contemplation, and by relying simply on your body, try to save yourself. Time means the action of human beings. The world may seem meaningless when viewed in the absence of time, or in the sweep of time, but when we consider the details and work upon them, it begins for the first time to possess boundless meaning. Wujing, place yourself in an appropriate situation, and devote yourself to appropriate work. As for the overarching question 'Why?' abandon it completely. If you do not, there can be no salvation.

"In the autumn of this year, three monks will cross this River of Flowing Sand, traveling from the east to the west. They are the monk Xuanzang, who is the reincarnation of the Venerable Elder Jinshan, Gold Cicada, of the western land, and two disciples. They have received an imperial command from the Tang emperor Taizong to journey to the Great Thunderclap Temple in India and to return with the original sutras of the Mahayana Tripitaka, the complete set of the Mahayana Buddhist scriptures. Wujing, you must accompany Xuanzang on his journey westward. This for you will be the appropriate situation and appropriate service. The passage may be arduous, but do not doubt; exert yourself in your duty forthrightly. One of Xuanzang's disciples is Sun Wukong. He is uneducated and ignorant, yet one who simply believes and has no doubt. You have much to learn from him."

The instruction complete, Wujing raised his head again. No one stood before him. In a daze, Wujing rose in the moonlight at the bottom of the river. It was a feeling he had not before experienced. In a corner of his foggy mind, he was thinking these rambling thoughts:

"To the creature to whom such things are likely to happen, such things happen; and when such things are likely to happen, such things happen. Half a year ago, I was not the kind of creature to dream such as I just have.... The words of the Bodhisattva in the dream, when I think about them, are not at all so different from the words of Master Nujushi or Master Dragon-Whiskered Catfish, yet tonight these words have touched my heart very deeply—it is uncanny. Of course, even I do not think that dreams can be the source of salvation. Yet while I do not understand why, I cannot help feeling strongly that it is possible that the Tang monk in the oracle would pass through this river. That is because, when such things are likely to happen, such things happen." Wujing thought of these things and smiled for the first time in a long while.

Seven

In the autumn of that year, as expected, Wujing received the grace of an encounter with the monk Xuanzang of the Great Tang; and by the powers of the master, Wujing was able to leave the watery world and be transformed into a human being. It then came to pass that he embarked upon a new journey of wanderings with the brave and innocent Sun Wukong, who was given the name "Great Sage, Equal to Heaven," as well as the lazy optimist Zhu Wuneng, who had once been known as Tian Peng, "Heavenly Reeds, Marshal of the Forces of the River of Heaven." But even after he began the journey, Wujing had not yet completely recovered from his old illness, and he did not give up his habit of talking to himself. He would mutter: "This is most peculiar. I do not understand. To stop forcing ourselves to ask questions about what we do not understand—is that what it means to understand? This is so ambiguous, so arbitrary. Not a very splendid sloughing off of the old self, is it? Hmm, hmm, . . . I am still not convinced. At any rate, I am indeed thankful, if only for the fact that things do not bother me as they once did."

Translated by Nobuko Ochner

Waxing and Waning

In the autumn of the thirty-ninth year of the reign of Duke Ling of Wei, Kuai Kui, the heir apparent, was ordered by his father to go on a mission to Qi. As he passed through the land of Song, he heard the farmers tilling their fields chant a strange refrain:

> *He's satisfied your sow already*
> *So now return our handsome boar.*

The heir apparent's face turned pale, for he knew what they were singing about. Nanzi, the wife of Duke Ling (but not the mother of Kuai Kui), was a native of Song. She had completely won over the duke, not so much by her beauty as by her cleverness, and recently she had urged him to appoint Lord Zhao, a gentleman from Song, to an official post in Wei. This Zhao was famed for his good looks. He had been involved in an immoral relationship with Nanzi prior to her coming as a bride to Wei, and this fact was known to everyone except Duke Ling himself. Now the relationship was being carried on quite openly at the Court of Wei. The "sow" and "boar" of which the peasants were singing were without doubt a reference to Nanzi and Zhao.

After Kuai Kui returned from his mission, he summoned the retainer Xi Yangsu and decided on a plan. When the heir apparent went to present his compliments to Lady Nanzi the next day, Xi Yangsu, armed with a dagger, was concealed behind a curtain in one corner of the room. As he spoke casually with Nanzi, Kuai Kui signaled with his eyes to his accomplice, but, perhaps out of fear, the would-be assassin did not emerge. The heir apparent signaled three times, but the only response was a slight movement of the black curtain. Meanwhile Lady Nanzi took notice of Kuai Kui's odd behavior. Following his glances, she became aware that someone was hiding in the room. She screamed and ran into an inner chamber.

Startled at the commotion, Duke Ling appeared. He took Nanzi's hand and tried to calm her, but she just kept repeating: "The heir apparent wants to kill me! The heir apparent wants to kill me!" The duke ordered his guardsmen to find Kuai Kui, but by then he and his accomplice had already fled far from the capital.

Kuai Kui went first to Song and then to Jin, telling everyone that his righteous rebellion, the killing of that licentious woman, had failed due to betrayal by the cowardly fool Xi Yangsu. When Xi heard this accusation, he responded: "What nonsense! I was within an inch of being betrayed by Kuai Kui. He used threats to make me try to kill his stepmother. Had I not agreed, I would surely have been killed; and if I had managed to kill her, I would have been blamed for the crime. Because I am prudent and knowledgeable about strategy, I agreed to Kuai Kui's proposal but did not carry out the murder."

Just then the state of Jin was in great turmoil due to a rebellion by the Fan and Zhonghang clans. The states of Qi and Wei were urging the rebels on, so the problem was not easily settled.

Kuai Kui, the heir apparent of Wei, lived in Jin under the protection of Zhao Jian, the main pillar of the state. Zhao's extraordinary kindness to Kuai Kui was due to his pleasure in defying the duke of Wei, who had shown himself to be against Jin.

Zhao was, as we have said, hospitable to Kuai Kui, but the status of the heir apparent in Jin was very different from what it had been in his native state. After three lonely years in the mountainous capital city Jiang, so different from the flat plains of his native Wei, he received news of his father's death. Rumor had it that, in the absence of the heir apparent, the duke had named Kuai Kui's own son, Che, as his heir. This was the son whom Kuai Kui had left behind when he fled Wei. This unsettled the exiled heir apparent, who had assumed that one of his half-brothers would be installed in his place. That child, as duke of Wei? When he recalled how immature his son had been only three years before, it seemed ludicrous. Kuai Kui would return at once to his native land and become duke of Wei himself. Nothing could be simpler!

The exiled heir apparent, supported by Zhao Jian's forces, crossed the Yellow River in high spirits. He was at last in Wei again! When he reached the town of Qi, however, it was clear that he could not take another step eastward since the new duke had refused him entry and had sent an army to lie in wait for him. Even to enter the town of Qi, the heir apparent had first to win the sympathy of the local people by wearing robes of mourning and bewailing his father's death. This made him angry, but there was no recourse. So he had managed to get one foot into a corner of his native state and now would have to remain there and wait for his opportunity.

He waited for thirteen years.

The duke, who was his son Che, whom he had doted upon, no longer existed for Kuai Kui. There was now only the greedy, hateful young duke of Wei who had stolen Kuai Kui's birthright and refused him entry to his native land. None of the officials whom Kuai Kui had favored in the past attempted to visit him to pay his respects. All were happy to work under the arrogant young duke and his adviser, the pompous and wily minister Kong Shuyu, who was in fact the husband of Kuai Kui's elder sister, and his own uncle. It was as if they had never heard the name of Kuai Kui.

In the thirteen years that Kuai Kui spent gazing at the waters of the Yellow River day and night, the capricious, self-indulgent, and in-experienced young aristocrat turned into a cruel, cynical middle-aged man who had seen too much of life.

His only consolation in the midst of this dreariness was his son Lord Ji, who was the younger half-brother of the present Duke Che, born to Kuai Kui of a different wife. As soon as his father entered Qi, Lord Ji hastened to his side, along with his mother, and the three lived together there. Kuai Kui was determined that, if he was ever able to regain the throne, Ji should be his heir. In his desperate state of mind, he also found diversion in the sport of cockfighting, which satisfied both his cruel urges and his love of gambling. At the same time, the sight of the strong, bold birds gave him intense aesthetic pleasure. He spent a good deal of his none-too-ample resources to build a row of splendid rooster-houses, where he raised the brave and beautiful birds.

Kong Shuyu, adviser to the young duke, died; and Boji, his widow, who was Kuai Kui's elder sister, took steps to ensure that her son Kong Kui would have no real power, taking the reins of government herself. Now, for the first time, the mood in the capital of Wei began to shift in favor of the exiled heir apparent. Boji's lover Hun Liangfu frequently traveled between the capital and Qi, bearing messages for Boji and Kuai Kui. The heir apparent made promises to Liangfu: when he gained the throne, he would appoint Liangfu to a high post, and even if Liangfu were guilty of a crime deserving death, Kuai Kui would forgive him as many as three times. Then, using Liangfu as his agent, Kuai Kui set about plotting his ascension to the throne with the greatest shrewdness.

In the fortieth year of the reign of King Jing of Zhou, on a certain day in the intercalary twelfth month, Kuai Kui was, after a long journey, welcomed into the Wei capital by Liangfu. At dusk, dressed as a woman, he snuck into the residence of the Kong clan, where, with the aid of his sister Boji and Liangfu, he issued threats against his nephew Kong Kui (Boji's son), who was the formal head of the Kong clan and the highest official in Wei. With Kong Kui as his unwilling "ally," Kuai Kui launched a coup d'etat. His son, the reigning duke of Wei, immediately fled, and Kuai Kui, the heir apparent (who was the reigning duke's father), assumed the throne as Duke Zhuang of Wei. Seventeen years had passed since he was driven from Wei by Lady Nanzi.

The new Duke Zhuang's first official acts involved neither changes in foreign relations nor the promotion of domestic governance. They were concerned, rather, with compensation for his wasted past or, one might say, revenge against that past. The pleasures that he could not enjoy during his time of misfortune he now required, at once and to the fullest measure. His self-respect, which had been crushed during his years of exile, now swelled to the point of arrogance. To those who had abused him in his time of trial, he applied the death sentence; to those who had scorned him, harsh punishment; to those who had shown no sympathy, calculated coldness.

His greatest regret was that Lady Nanzi, the consort of Duke Ling who had been the cause of his exile, had died the previous year, for his sweetest dream during his exile had been to get his hands on the adulteress and, after subjecting her to every humiliation, to execute her. To the great lords who had shown not the slightest interest in him in the past, he said, "I have tasted the bitterness of banishment for many years. What do you think? Would it not be good medicine for you all as well?" Of these great lords, there were not a few who fled the country at once.

It might have been expected that Kuai Kui would handsomely reward his elder sister Boji and nephew Kong Kui, who had helped him gain the throne. Yet one night, at a banquet he hosted, he made sure they got very drunk and loaded them into a carriage. He ordered the driver to take them, just as they were, beyond the frontiers of Wei.

Kuai Kui devoted his first year as duke of Wei to revenge, as one possessed. It should hardly be necessary to add that, to compensate for the unfulfilled years of his youth in exile, he scoured the capital for beautiful women, who were then taken into the Inner Palace.

As he had earlier decided, Kuai Kui made Lord Ji, who had shared the pain of exile with him, his heir apparent. He had thought of Ji as a mere boy, but now he had become a splendid figure of a young man. Perhaps because he had learned to read the secrets of the human heart in harsh times, Ji occasionally showed a streak of cruelty that was unsettling in one so young. The effects of Kuai Kui's excessive love for him as a boy now could be seen in the son's arrogance and the father's indulgence. The father showed a weakness of spirit that amazed on-lookers, but this was extended only toward his son. The heir apparent Ji and Liangfu, who had been promoted to high rank, were Duke Zhuang's only confidants.

One night, speaking with Hun Liangfu, Duke Zhuang mentioned that the former Duke Che had fled Wei taking with him the state's treasures dating from many earlier reigns. How, he asked Liangfu, might he go about recovering them? Liangfu ordered the candle bearers to leave the room and drew near the duke, holding a candle in his hand. In a low voice, he observed that both the exiled former Duke Che and the present heir apparent Ji were equally Duke Zhuang's sons. If the former had assumed the ducal dignity before his father, it was not because he himself had wished to do so. Why not take this opportunity to recall Che, compare his ability with that of Ji, and choose the more able as the proper heir? If Che proved to be untalented, Duke Zhuang could at that point simply confiscate the treasures he would have brought back with him to Wei....

It seems an informer was hiding in the room where this conversation took place. Despite Liangfu's attempts to ensure privacy before making this delicate proposal, the details at once became known to the heir apparent.

The next morning a livid Ji, accompanied by five men with their swords drawn, stormed into his father's chambers. Duke Zhuang, pale and trembling with fear, dared not rebuke his son for this rudeness. Ji had his retainers slaughter a boar, and forced his father to take a blood oath to guarantee Ji's status as heir apparent and to execute the duplicitous minister Liangfu. The duke protested that he had sworn to pardon Liangfu for three crimes deserving death. "Well then," Ji retorted, "you would surely execute him for a fourth offence, would you not?" Duke Zhuang, besieged and defenseless, could do nothing but agree.

In the spring of the next year, the duke built a pavilion at Jibu, a favorite resort in the suburbs, decorating the walls, utensils, and tapestries with tiger motifs. On the day of the opening ceremony, he hosted a lavish banquet to which all the notables of Wei came, dressed in fine silks. Hun Liangfu, who had originally been a mere court page, was now a "fashionable gentleman" fond of showy dress. For this occasion he wore a white fox fur coat over a purple robe, and was driven to the banquet in a carriage drawn by two stallions. Because the event was a casual affair, he did not bother to remove his sword before sitting at the dining table; and since he felt hot halfway through the dinner, he took off his fox-fur coat. Ji, the heir apparent, observing this behavior, rushed up, grabbed hold of his robe at chest-level, and pulled him up. Touching the tip of Liangfu's nose with his naked sword-blade, Ji upbraided him: "You carry your rudeness too far, varlet, presuming on your lord's kindness! On his behalf, I will execute you here and now!"

Liangfu had no confidence in his ability to fight, so he did not attempt to resist, but only cast an imploring look at Duke Zhuang as he cried out: "My lord, you promised to forgive me three capital offenses! So even if I have been guilty of offense today, the heir apparent should not be allowed to raise his sword against me."

"Three offenses?" said the heir apparent. "Let us count them! You are wearing a purple robe, but purple is the prerogative of the sovereign —that is one. You arrived in a carriage drawn by two stallions, like a high official directly serving under the Emperor—that is two. You took off your coat in the presence of your lord and ate without removing your sword—that is three."

"That is only three—you cannot kill me!" pleaded Liangfu, as he struggled violently in Ji's grip.

"No, there is more! Have you forgotten what you said to your lord? You are an evil minister, trying to set your lords, who are father and son, against each other!"

Liangfu's face turned white as a sheet of paper.

"So, your crimes are four!" Before the heir apparent had finished this sentence, Liangfu's head toppled forward, his blood spurting onto the great tapestry embroidered with fierce tigers in gold thread against a black background.

In ashen-faced silence Duke Zhuang watched what his son had done.

A message came to Duke Zhuang from Zhao Jian in Jin. Its burden was that, when the Duke was in exile, the Court of Jin had done its best to help him, inadequate though that may have been; yet Duke Zhuang had sent no word of greeting since his return to Wei. If the duke himself were too busy, could he not at least dispatch the heir apparent to present formal greetings to the duke of Jin? Hearing these rather imperious words, Duke Zhuang recalled the misery of his past, and considered the message a blow to his pride. He replied, saying that, due to the unsettled conditions in his state, he wished to postpone his formal greetings.

Immediately afterward, a secret message arrived at the court of Jin. It was from the heir apparent of Wei, advising the duke of Jin not to believe his father's reply, which was mere evasion: Duke Zhuang had postponed sending formal greetings because he felt uneasy about Jin, in whose debt he stood. This was obviously a ploy on the heir apparent's part to enable him to succeed his father as quickly as possible; realizing this, Zhao Jian felt some discomfort. Still, he thought it absolutely necessary to punish the duke of Wei for his ingratitude.

One autumn night that year, Duke Zhuang had a disturbing dream. On a barren plain, an old tower stood, its eaves aslant. A lone man climbed the tower and, tossing his head of hair wildly, loudly exclaimed: "I see them, I see them! I see a whole field of melons!" The plain seemed oddly familiar, and even in the dream the duke realized it was the ruins of a settlement of the Kunwu clan. Indeed, there were heaps of large melons everywhere. "Who could have raised the little melons to such a great size?" the man went on. "And who could have safeguarded the pitiful exile until he turned into the flourishing duke of Wei?" Duke Zhuang, yet dreaming, seemed to recognize the voice of the man shouting and stamping his feet like a madman there on the tower. He strained his ears, and now it became utterly clear who it was: "I am Hun Liangfu! What was my crime? What was my crime?"

Duke Zhuang awoke in a cold sweat. He felt awful. He stepped out onto the balcony. A late moon had just risen over the edge of the plain. It was a muddy reddish moon, close to copper in color. The duke, troubled that this was a bad omen, returned to his sleeping chamber and took up the oracle sticks by the light of the night lamp.

The next morning he summoned an oracle-reader and had him judge the omens. Nothing harmful, was the verdict. Delighted, the duke rewarded the oracle-reader with land. But no sooner had the oracle-reader left the duke's presence than he fled Wei to another state. Had he read the omens truthfully, he knew he would suffer for it; therefore he decided to deceive the duke, glossing the matter over, and then flee as quickly as he could.

The duke next tried divination by using a tortoise-shell. Consulting a text that interpreted omens, he found this passage: "The fish is tired and ill. It drags its red tail and floats on its side in the current, moving listlessly near the shore. A great state will destroy it; and, truly, it will soon perish. It closes the city gates and the water gates, and seeks to pass over the rear one." The duke understood the "great state" to be a reference to Jin, but was unsure what the rest of the text meant. Nonetheless, it seemed certain that his future as duke of Wei would be dark. Aware that his time was short, Duke Zhuang took no strong measures against Jin or the arrogance of his heir apparent; instead, he hastened to indulge in as many pleasures as he could before the gloomy prophecy was fulfilled. Large-scale building was undertaken continually, requiring massive forced labor of the harshest sort, and the resentful voices of the master-builders and stonemasons filled the city streets.

The duke's passion for cockfighting, which he had temporarily forgotten, revived. Now, unlike in his days of obscurity, he could indulge this taste without restraint. Making full use of the money and power he possessed, he collected the finest birds from within and without his domains. There was one cock in particular, bought from a nobleman of Lu, whose feathers were like gold and whose spurs like steel; with its tall comb and long, erect tail-feathers, it was without doubt a rare specimen. There might be days when the duke did not set foot in the women's Inner Palace, but there was never a day when he did not go to observe this splendid cock fluffing out its feathers and flapping its wings.

One day, as the duke gazed down on the city from a palace tower, an extremely crowded, squalid area of the city caught his notice. An attendant explained that this was the district inhabited by foreigners: members of a different race who were descended from an uncivilized people far to the west. The duke ordered that the district be torn down because it was unsightly and that the foreigners be expelled to a site ten li outside the city gates. With their children on their backs and their elderly trailing behind them, and with their meager belongings heaped onto carts, the wretched foreigners filed out of the city, harried along by city officials. It was a scene that could be clearly observed from the palace towers.

Among the crowd being forced from the city, one woman with extraordinarily beautiful long hair stood out. At once the duke had the woman brought to him. She was the wife of one of the foreigners, belonging to a clan known as the "Ji," and while her face was not particularly attractive, her hair was luxuriant. Wanting a wig for one of his favorite concubines, the duke ordered that the woman's hair be shorn at the roots.

The woman, now bald, was returned to the line of deportees, and her husband hurriedly covered her head with a veil, then turned to glare at the figure of the duke, standing in his tower high above them. Even the whips of the city officials did not easily drive him from that spot.

That winter, as the Jin army invaded from the west, an official named Shi Bu raised an army within Wei and attacked the ducal palace. Shi Bu had learned of Duke Zhuang's intent to remove him from office and decided to strike first; but many also believed that this was part of a conspiracy involving the heir apparent.

Duke Zhuang closed all the city gates and, climbing to the top of one of the towers, addressed the rebel army himself, offering various terms for peace. Shi Bu, however, refused to reply. The duke was left, as night fell, to guard the city with a small band of soldiers under his direct command.

The duke was forced to flee under cover of darkness, before the moon rose. Accompanied by a few nobles and retainers, and carrying in his arms his beloved "tall-combed, lofty-tailed" cock, he needed to scale the rear gate of the city. Unused to climbing, he lost his footing and fell, suffering a blow to the thigh and spraining his ankle. There was no time to treat the injuries. Helped along by his retainers, he hurried across the dark plain. He was determined to cross the border into Song before dawn.

After the party had walked for some time, the sky seemed suddenly to float up, dimly yellow, away from the blackness of the plain. The moon had risen. It was a muddy, copper-colored moon, exactly like the moon over the palace balcony the night he had woken from his dream. "A bad sign," thought the duke, and in that instant, black shadows sprang from the tall grass around them and attacked. Were they bandits or pursuers? He had no time to think; he had to fight for his life. The members of his entourage were almost all killed, but the duke managed to crawl to safety through the tall grass. He may have escaped precisely because he could not stand.

He realized that he was still holding the cock tightly. It had not crowed even once during the melee, but that was because it was long since dead. Still, the duke could not bring himself to toss the dead creature away, and he continued to crawl through the grass with the cock in one hand.

In one corner of the plain, the duke caught sight of what seemed, strangely enough, to be a small settlement. The duke dragged himself there and, gasping for breath, crawled up to the first house he reached. After he was helped indoors and given a cup of water, he heard a deep voice cry out, "At last you've come!" Taken aback, the duke looked up to see a man with prominent buckteeth and a reddish face staring down at him. He had no memory of such a face. "You don't remember me? Probably not. But I bet you remember her!" the man said. He beckoned to a woman crouching in the corner. When the duke made out the woman's face in the dim lamplight, he let the corpse of the rooster fall from his hand and nearly collapsed. The woman, wearing a veil over her head, was the wife of the foreign clansman, and it was her hair that the duke had stolen to make a wig for his favorite concubine.

"Forgive me," the duke said hoarsely. "Forgive me, please."

With trembling hands, he removed the precious gems he had twined around his waist and offered them to the clansman. "I will give you these. Only let me go, please, I beg you!"

The man unsheathed his curved sword as he drew near the duke. "You think the jewels will disappear when I kill you?" he sneered.

In this way did Kuai Kui, Duke of Wei, meet his end.

≈ Translated by Paul McCarthy

Li Ling

One

In the ninth lunar month of Tianhan 2 (99 BCE), during the reign of Emperor Wu of the Han dynasty, Commander of the Cavalry Li Ling led a force of five thousand foot-soldiers north from the border fort of Zheluzhang. For thirty days, they threaded their way through harsh foothills where the southeastern end of the Altai mountain range starts to give way to the Gobi Desert. The cold north wind cut through their uniforms, and they felt truly isolated, ten thousand *li* from any source of help. When they reached the foothills of Mount Xunji at the northern edge of the Gobi Desert, the army at last made camp. They were already deep inside the territories of their enemy, the Xiongnu nomads, known to the West as "the Huns." It being so far north, the clover had withered, and the elms and willows had shed all their leaves, although it was still autumn. Even the trees themselves were hard to find, apart from the area surrounding the camp, so harsh and wild was the landscape, with nothing but sand and rocks and a waterless riverbed. As far as the eye could see, there were no signs of human habitation. The only signs of life were the occasional antelope that ventured onto the plain in search of water, and formations of wild geese flying south high above the distant mountains clearly outlined against the autumn sky. Yet not a single man was moved to sweet nostalgic thoughts of home. Their situation was too perilous to permit that.

To move against the Xiongnu—whose cavalry was their main force—with infantry alone, without even a single company of horsemen (the only mounted men being Li Ling and a few adjutants), and to push deep into enemy territory—this was the height of folly! The infantry, moreover, numbered a mere five thousand, without possible reinforcements, and Mount Xunji was a full thousand five hundred *li* from the nearest Han fort at Juyan. It would have been impossible to continue such a march without his men having absolute trust in Li Ling as commander.

Every year when the autumn winds began to blow, a horde of bold and fierce invaders would appear, whipping their northern horses on as they raced through the northern borderlands of the Han territories. They slaughtered the officials, plundered the people, and made off with their cattle. Year after year towns like Wuyuan, Shuofang, Yunzhong, Shanggu, and Yanmen became victims. For thirty years these calamities continued to befall the northern frontier, except for the few years from 122 to 111 BCE, when it was said that, for a time, owing to the successful strategies of Generalissimo Wei Qing and General Huo Qubing, who was known as "the Strong and Swift," there were no Xiongnu towns south of the Gobi. But Huo Qubing had died eighteen years before, and Wei Qing, seven years.

Zhao Ponu, known as "the Hammer of the Huns," who had earlier been appointed lord of Zhuoye for his services, was taken prisoner along with his whole army; and the defensive fortifications built in the north by Xu Ziwei, Commander of the Palace Gates, were immediately destroyed by the Xiongnu. There was one Han commander left who had the respect of the entire army: General Li Guangli, who had made a great name for himself by leading an expedition against Ferghana several years before.

In the summer of that year—Tianhan 2—in the fifth lunar month, General Li Guangli left Jiuquan at the head of thirty thousand cavalry, well before the Xiongnu invasion. He planned to attack the Xiongnu commander, Lord Youxian, who was watching for an opportunity to invade the western frontier, near the Tian mountain range.

Emperor Wu ordered Li Ling to take charge of provisioning the army's campaign. When he was summoned to the Wutai Hall of the palace, however, Li Ling earnestly begged to be excused from that task. He was the grandson of the famous Li Guang, known as "the Flying Arrow" due to his skill in archery. Li Ling himself was an expert at mounted archery and had long been said to resemble his grandfather in that respect; for some years past, he had been stationed at Jiuquan and Zhangye in the west, in charge of training the troops in archery. He was close to forty years of age, at the height of his powers, and the job of provisioning the troops must have seemed beneath him. Since the troops he was now training in the borderlands were superb soldiers from Jing and Qu, he implored the Emperor that he be permitted to lead them out to attack and contain the Xiongnu army.

Emperor Wu was inclined to grant this request. Unfortunately, he said, he had no cavalry reserves to spare for Li Ling's forces, since the cavalry had been dispatched to so many different areas already. Li Ling responded that it didn't matter. It must have seemed an impossible task to accomplish under those conditions; but so distasteful was the proposed job of provisioning that he would rather take the risk together with his five thousand troops, who would not hesitate to give their lives for his sake. "I would like to attack a great force with my small one!" he proclaimed. Emperor Wu, who had always liked such shows of valor, was highly pleased with Li Ling's words and granted his request.

Having returned to Zhangye in the west, Li Ling readied his troops and set out at once for the north. Lu Bode, Commander of the Crossbow Troops, who was then encamped at Juyan, was ordered to go out and meet Li Ling's army at the halfway point. That was all well and good, but then things took a very serious turn for the worse.

Lu Bode had served under General Huo Qubing for many years and had been enfeoffed as lord of Pili. He was a veteran who, as naval commander, had with one hundred thousand troops succeeded in destroying southern Yue twelve years earlier. After becoming implicated in some illegality, however, he had lost his fief and been demoted to his present position of guarding the western frontiers. Between him and Li Ling, the difference in age was like that of father and son. For this veteran general, who had formerly been an enfeoffed lord, to yield pride of place to the younger Li Ling was hard to swallow. At the very time that he went to greet Li and his army, he was sending a messenger to the capital to raise strategic objections. He pointed out that, since it was autumn, the Xiongnu's horses were well fed and sturdy; and that with so few soldiers it would be difficult for Li Ling to bear the brunt of their attacks, skilled as the Xiongnu were in battle on horseback. Therefore, Lu Bode argued, it would be better if both Li Ling and he passed the New Year where they were and, after spring came, carried out sorties from Zhiuquan and Zhangye with five thousand horsemen each. Such was his message to the emperor, a message of which Li Ling was entirely unaware.

When Emperor Wu read it, he was furious, thinking it the product of discussions between Lu Bode and Li Ling. "What is the meaning of this? Boasting to my face of what he will do, then going to the frontier and getting cold feet!" A courier was sent posthaste from the capital to where Lu Bode and Li Ling were encamped. To Lu Bode, the message was: "Li Ling boasted in my presence of wishing to attack the many with a few. There is therefore no need for you to assist him. The Xiongnu have just invaded Xihe, and you, Bode, are to leave Li Ling where he is and hasten to Xihe to block the enemy's path."

The Emperor's message to Li Ling was: "Go at once to the north Gobi and observe any developments from Mount Xunji in the east to the Longle River in the south. If there is nothing amiss, proceed to the town of Shouxiang, following the route used by the lord of Zhuoye in the past, and rest your men." It goes without saying that the emperor appended furious questions about "the outrageous message you sent me after conferring with Bode!"

For an army without horses, the march of several thousand li was brutal, quite apart from the dangers of wandering about enemy territory with so few troops. This would be obvious to anyone who took into account the time required for such a march on foot, the need for hauling the military wagons by manpower alone, and the climate of the nomads' territory as winter drew on. Emperor Wu was by no means a mediocre ruler, and he had the same strengths and weaknesses as Emperor Yang of Sui and the First Emperor of Qin, who were, likewise, decisive monarchs. Even General Li Guangli, the elder brother of Emperor Wu's most beloved consort, aroused the emperor's ire when he sought to retreat for a time from Ferghana because he lacked sufficient manpower: to prevent the general's return, the emperor ordered that the frontier at Yumenguan be closed. The campaign against Ferghana itself was occasioned by the emperor's desire to acquire the best-quality horses, and nothing more. Once the emperor set his mind on something, he was not to be deterred, no matter what the cost.

In this case, moreover, the onus was on Li Ling, since he himself had asked to be given the task. He therefore had no reason to hesitate, despite the great difficulties posed by the season and distances. And so Li Ling set off on his "northern campaign sans cavalry."

Li Ling's forces stayed at Mount Xunji for ten days, and each day scouts were sent out near and far to learn what the enemy was doing. But Li Ling also had to report to the capital on the geography of the area, supplying maps showing mountains and rivers. This intelligence was given to Chen Bule, one of his subordinates, who put the materials carefully inside his tunic, bowed to Li Ling, then mounted one of the fewer than ten horses available, and with a flick of his riding crop galloped off down the hill to make his way alone to the capital. With heavy hearts, the officers and men watched his figure grow smaller and smaller, disappearing into the vastness of the dry gray landscape.

During the ten days at Mount Xunji, Li Ling and his forces did not see even one Xiongnu soldier in the space of thirty *li* to the east and to the west.

General Li Guangli had gone to attack the enemy in the Tian mountain range in the summer, leaving well before the arrival of Li Ling's forces. Although he defeated Lord Youxian on one occasion, on his return from that battle he found himself surrounded by a different Xiongnu army and was overwhelmed. Six or seven out of ten Han troops were killed, and the general himself was endangered.

When this news reached Li Ling, he wondered where this main body of the enemy troops might be now. There was an enemy force that was currently being held in check by General Gongsun Ao around Xihe and Shuofang (Lu Bode had rushed to his aid there after leaving Li Ling); but, considering the time and distance involved, it seemed unlikely that these were the enemy's main force that had overwhelmed Li Guangli.

It seemed impossible that they would have moved so swiftly from the Tian mountain range to the Ordos high plain, which was some four thousand *li* to the east. No, the Xiongnu's main force must now be encamped in the area between Li Ling's position and the Zhiju River to the north. Everyday Li Ling stood atop the mountain in front of his camp and looked in all four directions. From the east to the south there was nothing but an expanse of desolate flat desert; from the west to the north, low mountains and hills with few trees stretched on and on. Occasionally he caught sight of either a hawk or a falcon soaring among the autumn clouds, but he never saw even a single nomad horseman come riding over the earth.

Li Ling arranged the army wagons in a circle at the edge of a sparsely forested gorge, and he set up his headquarters inside it. When night came, the temperature dropped precipitately. The men cut down what few trees there were to burn for warmth. During their ten days' encampment, the moon disappeared from the sky. The stars were incredibly beautiful, perhaps due to the dryness of the air. Each night Sirius sent a slanting bluish-white radiance against the pitch-black shadow of the mountains.

They had spent more than ten peaceful days when Li Ling decided it was time to move southeast along the appointed route. The night before they were due to depart, a sentry was gazing up at the brilliant form of Sirius, when all at once there appeared another, extremely large, reddish star beneath it. As the sentry watched in amazement, this new, large star began to move, dragging behind it a thick red tail. Then there were two, three, four, five similar lights in the same vicinity, also moving. As the sentry was about to cry out, those distant lights all at once disappeared. It was as if he had been seeing them in a dream.

When he heard the sentry's report, Li Ling ordered the entire army to prepare for battle at dawn. He inspected each battalion and then returned to his tent and fell fast asleep, emitting thunderous snores.

Early the next morning, he found that his troops had mustered as ordered and were quietly awaiting the enemy. The soldiers were sent beyond the circle of army wagons: troops with pikes and shields were placed in the front rank, those with bows and crossbows in the rear. The two mountains that flanked the valley were silent in the darkness just before dawn, but the men sensed danger hidden beneath the surrounding crags.

As the morning sun began to penetrate the valleys (the Xiongnu would not take action until their khan had worshiped the rising sun), from the summits to the slopes of the mountains, where hitherto nothing had been visible, innumerable human figures suddenly emerged. With shouts that seemed to shake the heavens and the earth, the barbarians rushed down the mountainsides. When the first onslaught had come within twenty paces, a roll of drums echoed from within the Han camp, which until then had been absolutely silent. A thousand crossbows fired at once, and several hundred of the Xiongnu fell to the ground. Without a moment's delay, the Han army's front rank of halberdsmen attacked the remaining barbarians, who had been stunned by the rain of arrows. Completely routed, the Xiongnu army fled back up the mountainsides. The Han forces pursued, taking barbarian heads in the thousands.

It was a splendid victory, but the tenacious enemy would certainly not withdraw, leaving things as they were. There must have been thirty thousand enemy troops flung into battle on that day alone. And, judging from the banners that floated on the hilltops, they were the Xiongnu khan's personal guards. If the khan were there, the Han army would have to expect a rearguard of eighty thousand to one hundred thousand sent out in wave after wave of attacks.

Li Ling decided immediately to withdraw and move south. The previous day's plan to go to Shouxiang, two thousand *li* to the southeast, was abandoned. Instead, the army would travel south along the same route they had come two weeks earlier, and try to return to Fort Juyan as speedily as possible (although it too was well over a thousand *li* distant).

On the afternoon of the third day of their southward journey, a cloud of yellow dust could be seen rising up far to the rear of the Han forces, on the northern horizon. The Xiongnu cavalry were in pursuit. By the next day some eighty thousand nomad troops had seamlessly surrounded the Han army on every side, so fast were their horses; but stung, it seemed, by their defeat a few days earlier, they did not venture too close. They loosely circled the Han army, their mounted archers sending volleys of arrows from a distance. When Li Ling ordered his army to halt and prepare to engage the enemy, the Xiongnu would ride some little distance away, avoiding pitched battle. When the Han forces resumed their march, the Xiongnu would ride closer and let loose their arrows.

Thus the pace of the march was greatly slowed, and the number of dead and wounded grew steadily day by day. Like wolves pursuing a starving, exhausted traveler through the wilderness, the Xiongnu tracked the Han troops, always using the same tactic. They would wound and weaken the Han little by little, watching for a chance to move in for the kill.

For several days, the two forces moved south, now fighting, now retreating, until the Han decided to rest for one day in a mountain valley. The number of wounded was already quite large. Li Ling took a roll call to determine how bad the situation was and then he decided as follows: soldiers with just a single wound would be required to bear arms and fight as usual; soldiers with two wounds would help push the army wagons; and soldiers with three wounds or more would be placed on hand-carts and transported by their fellow soldiers. The bodies of the dead would have to be abandoned in the wilderness.

That night during camp inspection, Li Ling happened to discover a woman dressed in men's clothing hiding in one of the supply carts. Inspection of all the supply carts revealed the presence of over ten women similarly hidden. Several years earlier, a robber band from Guangdong had been caught and killed, and their women and children had managed to flee to these western regions. Some of the widows, lacking food and clothing, had married border guards; not a few of the others had become prostitutes, servicing the Han troops. These women had secreted themselves in the military carts and accompanied the troops all the way to the northern desert. Li Ling promptly ordered his officers to kill the women.

Nothing whatever was said about the officers and men whose companions they were. The women were taken to a hollow in the valley, and for a time the echo of their high-pitched wailing was heard. Then all at once it ceased, as if swallowed up in the night's silence. The men within the camp stood, gravely listening.

The next morning the Han army fought with brave determination against the enemy who, after a long interval, now dared to attack at close quarters. But the Xiongnu left behind over three thousand corpses on the battlefield that day. The Han army, who were exasperated by the protracted guerilla warfare that the Xiongnu had been waging, found that their long-suppressed fighting spirit had suddenly reasserted itself.

The next day the Han army's retreat toward the south began again, following the old road to Longcheng. The Xiongnu, for their part, reverted to their original tactic of distant encirclement. On the fifth day, the Han troops entered one of the marshes that are sometimes found among the desert sands. The water of the marsh was half frozen, and the mud reached to the soldiers' knees. There seemed no end to the expanse of dry reeds through which they marched.

A party of Xiongnu that had gone upwind of them set fire to the reeds. A north wind fanned the flames; and the fire, burning white and giving off no light under the noonday sun, advanced toward the Han with terrifying speed. Li Ling at once ordered his men to set fire to the reeds near them and so narrowly managed to stop the oncoming flames. The fire was averted, but the difficulties in pushing the army wagons and carts through the quagmire were indescribable.

After slogging through the mud the whole night without finding a place to rest, they at last reached higher ground in the morning, only to meet with attack by the enemy's main force, which had circled ahead and was lying in ambush for them. What followed was a wild free-for-all of men and horses. Trying to evade the nomads' fierce cavalry attack, Li Ling abandoned the supply carts and shifted the battleground to the sparsely forested foothills.

The rain of arrows let loose by the Han forces from among the trees had a dramatic effect. The khan and his personal guards appeared at the head of their troops, and a hail of arrows descended upon them. The khan's white horse reared up, its forelegs pawing the air, throwing the blue-clad barbarian king to the ground. Two of his mounted guards swept him up from either side, and the whole brigade at once surrounded him and galloped off. After hours of intense combat, the Han were able to fight off their tenacious enemy, but it had been their hardest battle to date. The enemy had again left several thousand corpses on the battlefield, but the Han army too had lost close to a thousand men.

From the mouth of a Xiongnu prisoner taken that day, Li Ling learned something of the situation in the enemy camp: The khan was amazed at the toughness of the Han forces, apparently unafraid of a massive army twenty times their own. They seemed to be inviting him to follow as they made their way south day by day. He suspected there might be a hidden Han force somewhere nearby, on whose help they were relying. The previous night the khan had discussed this with his principal officers. They agreed that it was plausible, but concluded that if the khan, leading several tens of thousands of cavalry, could not destroy the small Han force, it would mean a terrible loss of face. Thus, the war party prevailed, and it was decided to attack relentlessly as the Han moved southward through the next forty to fifty *li* of mountains and valleys. When they emerged into the flatlands, the Xiongnu would launch a decisive battle. If even then they could not prevail against the Han, it would be time to send the troops back to the north.

Hearing this account from the enemy prisoner, Han Yannian and the other commanders of the Han army felt the first faint stirrings of hope that they might emerge from this alive.

Beginning the next day, the nomad attacks were extraordinarily intense. This must be the start of the final string of assaults that the prisoner had spoken of, they thought. There were repeated attacks, well over ten times per day. Fiercely counter-attacking, the Han army moved steadily southward. After three days, they entered the plains. Now that the battle was to be on level ground, the Xiongnu, taking advantage of the greatly increased power of their cavalry, attacked furiously; but once again they were forced to retreat, leaving two thousand dead behind. If what the prisoner had said was true, the nomad army could be expected now to give up their pursuit of the Han. Since it was only the word of a single captured soldier, it could not be fully relied on; but even so, the commanders felt somewhat relieved—that was undeniable.

That evening a Han scout named Guan Gan slipped out of the camp and went over to the Xiongnu. The night before, this Guan Gan, who had been a young hooligan in Chang'an, was rebuked and whipped in front of the troops by Han Yannian for neglect of duty. That was why he had deserted, but some also said that one of the women killed in the valley several days before had been his wife. Now Guan Gan knew what the Xiongnu prisoner had told the Han officers, so when he was brought into the presence of the khan, he said the following: There was no hidden Han army, and therefore no need for the Xiongnu to withdraw out of fear of one. There were no reinforcements for the Han troops, and their arrows were almost gone. Many of the soldiers had been wounded, and it would be grueling for the army to keep on marching. The core of the Han army consisted of two groups of eight hundred men led by General Li Ling and Commander Han Yannian. They were designated by yellow and white banners, so if the pick of the Xiongnu cavalry were to concentrate their attacks on those two groups tomorrow and defeat them, the rest of the Han army would easily be crushed.

He told all this to the khan, who was greatly pleased and rewarded Guan Gan accordingly. The khan then at once revoked his order for withdrawal to the north.

The next day, the pick of the nomad cavalry attacked, charging toward the yellow and white banners and shouting for Li Ling and Han Yannian's immediate surrender. The Han army was gradually pushed back from the plain to the mountainous area to the west and finally driven into a valley far from the main route. The enemy poured down arrows like rain from the surrounding mountaintops. The Han no longer had any arrows to shoot back. The five hundred thousand arrows—one hundred per soldier—with which the army had left Zheluzhang, had all been expended, and half of the other weaponry—swords, spears, pikes, and halberds—was damaged and useless. It was as the saying has it: "With swords broken and arrows spent."

Even so, those who had lost their pikes cut spokes from the wagon wheels to use instead, and civilian officials prepared to defend themselves with their short swords. The valley got narrower and narrower as they proceeded deeper into it. The enemy troops hurled huge rocks down from the crags, and this proved more effective in inflicting death and injury than mere arrows could have. Mounds of corpses and piles of rocks made further progress impossible.

That night Li Ling changed into a tight-sleeved simple tunic and, forbidding anyone to come along, left the encampment by himself. The moon hung low over the ravine, shedding its light on the piled-up corpses in the valley. It had been dark the night the army left camp at Mount Xunji, but the moon had now begun to get brighter. The moonlight and the frost covering the ground made one side of the steep valley look wet with water. The officers and men, who remained within the camp, surmised from the way Li Ling was dressed that he planned to spy on the enemy camp and, if the chance presented itself, to engage the khan in a fight to the death.

Li Ling did not come back for a long time. The men listened for sounds from outside the camp, hardly daring to breathe. The notes of a reed flute echoed from the enemy camp far above them. After a long while, the flap of the tent where the men were gathered was silently raised, and Li Ling entered. "It's no good," he spat out, sitting down on a camp stool. After a while, he said to no one in particular: "There's nothing for it but to let the whole army die fighting." No one said a word.

Minutes passed, before a civilian official ventured to say that when Zhao Ponu, the lord of Zhuoye, had been taken prisoner by the Xiongnu some years before and then fled back to the Han territories several years later, Emperor Wu had not punished him. This would suggest that even if Li Ling, having struck terror into the hearts of the Xiongnu with such a small force, should flee back to the capital now, the emperor would surely reward him.

Li Ling interrupted him: "Leave me aside for the moment! If we had any arrows, we might be able to break through the enemy encirclement; but with not even one arrow, at dawn tomorrow the entire army will have to surrender. If, however, we break out tonight, and everyone scatters and flees pell-mell, someone might make it to a border fort and be able to send a report to the emperor. I think we are now in the mountainous region north of Mount Tihan, still several days' journey to Juyuan, so success is very unlikely. Even so, at this point it's the only course left to us."

The commanders nodded in agreement. The officers and men were each given two measures of dried grain and a chunk of ice and instructed to run as fast as they could toward Zheluzhang. At the same time, the camp battle-flags were taken down, ripped up, and buried, and all weapons and military wagons that might be of use to the enemy were destroyed. Around midnight the order was given to beat the drums to wake the troops, but the drums failed to resound—it was a bad omen. Li Ling and Han Yannian mounted their horses and led the way, attended by some ten well-hardened mounted troops. The plan was to break through the eastern end of the valley into which they had been driven, emerge onto the plain, and then race south.

The new moon had already set. Taking the Xiongnu by surprise, two-thirds of the army managed to break through the eastern end of the valley. They were immediately set upon by the enemy cavalry, however. Most of the Han foot-soldiers were killed or captured; but several dozen were able in the confusion of battle to steal Xiongnu horses, which they whipped on, galloping southward.

Li Ling took a count of his men who had managed to shake off the pursuing enemy and escape over the expanse of sand, vaguely white even in the night. Having determined that they numbered over one hundred, he returned to the scene of carnage at the entrance to the valley. He had sustained several wounds, and his battle-dress was sodden with blood—his own and that of his foes. Han Yannian, who had been fighting alongside him, was dead. Having lost his officers and indeed his whole army, Li Ling could not bear the thought of facing the emperor. Taking up his halberd again, he rushed back into the thick of battle. In the darkness it was hard to tell friend from foe in the melee. Suddenly his horse fell forward, struck by a random arrow. At almost the same moment, Li Ling drew his spear back to stab an enemy in front of him and was struck by a heavy blow on the head from behind. He tumbled off his horse, unconscious, and a mass of Xiongnu soldiers piled on top of him, hoping to take him alive.

Two

The five-thousand-strong Han army that had set out for the north in the ninth month had been reduced to a defeated group of fewer than four hundred soldiers—weary, wounded, and without their general— when in the eleventh month they reached a fort on the frontier. News of their defeat quickly reached the capital of Chang'an via post-horse.

Emperor Wu was not as angry as might have been expected. Given that the main Han army, a large force commanded by Li Guangli, had been soundly defeated earlier, it was unreasonable to expect much from Li Ling's small force, amounting to a single detachment. Moreover, the emperor was convinced that Li Ling had died in battle. Nonetheless, Chen Bule, who had earlier come from the northern deserts bearing a message from Li Ling to the effect that all was quiet on the battlefront and the troops' spirits were high, and who had been rewarded with an official post for having brought such good tidings, and remained even now in the capital—this Chen Bule had of necessity to commit suicide. Everyone felt sorry for him, but there was no help for it.

In spring of the following year, Tianhan 3, news arrived at the capital that Li Ling had not died in battle but had been captured and was being held prisoner. Now Emperor Wu was furious. He was close to sixty, having then reigned for over forty years, but he was more hot-tempered even than in his prime. He loved tales of gods and immortals and had deep faith in diviners and shamans, by whom he had several times been deceived over the years. This great emperor, who exercised power for a total of over fifty years while the Han dynasty was at its height, had since his middle years had an obsessive, uneasy interest in the supernatural world. Thus, disappointments in that realm were all the more telling blows to him. As he grew older, a succession of such blows had made him—a person by nature quite open-hearted—darkly suspicious of his officials. Three successive prime ministers—Li Cai, Qing Zhai, and Zhao Zhou—were each put to death. The present prime minister, Gongsun He, had actually wept openly in front of the emperor, fearful of what would happen to him after he accepted his appointment. Ever since the resolute minister Ji An retired, the emperor had been surrounded by flatterers or corrupt, cruel men.

Emperor Wu summoned the various high officials to discuss what should be done about Li Ling. The general himself was not physically present in the capital, of course; but if his guilt was decided, his wife, children, and relatives were available for punishment and his property liable to seizure. One legal official, known for his cruelty, was skilled at reading the emperor's face and bending the law to accord with the ruler's wishes. When someone reproved him for this, citing the authority of the law, he replied: "What earlier rulers approved becomes the law, and what a later ruler approves becomes the regulation. What law can there be, apart from the will of the ruler?"

All the ministers were cut from the same cloth as this legal official. No one, from Prime Minister Gongsun He, Superintendent of the Court of Impeachment Du Zhou, and Superintendent of Rites Zhao Di on down, would attempt to defend Li Ling at the risk of incurring the emperor's wrath. They denounced his traitorous behavior. They said how embarrassed they were ever to have served at court alongside such a turncoat. Everyone agreed that, in retrospect, Li Ling's overall conduct had been suspect. The charge that Ling's cousin Li Gan had grown haughty because he had the favor of the crown prince became an excuse for baseless accusations against Ling himself. Those who were the most favorably inclined toward Ling simply kept their mouths closed and did not criticize him, but even they were few in number.

There was just one man who watched these developments with a pained countenance. Were these men who were slandering Li Ling now not the same as those who had, some months earlier, toasted his departure from the capital, offering him the highest encouragement? And were they not precisely the same men who had, when the messenger arrived from the northern deserts with the news that all was well with Li Ling's forces, praised the small army's fighting spirit, declaring Li Ling a worthy grandson of the great General Li Guang? This single observer wondered at these high officials, who pretended to have quite forgotten all that had gone before, and also at the emperor himself, who was wise enough to see through the officials' sycophancy yet refused to lend an ear to the truth. No—he did not actually "wonder at" this, since he knew all too well from long experience that this is what people were like. But even so, it remained distasteful to him.

As a middle-ranking official at court, he too was asked for his opinion. In his reply, he made a point of praising Li Ling. He remarked that, when one observed Ling's conduct, one could see that he was filial in serving his parents, trustworthy in his relations with other gentlemen, and a true patriot in his readiness to stand up, cast aside concern for his own safety, and sacrifice himself when the nation was in crisis. Now, alas, he had suffered a defeat; but how truly unfortunate it was that the emperor's wise judgment should be in danger of being obscured by the accusations of flattering courtiers whose only wish was to preserve themselves and safeguard their wives and children, and who were now taking advantage of Ling's one failure, which they distorted and exaggerated. Ling, after all, had led a force of fewer than five thousand foot-soldiers deep into enemy territory, nearly exhausted the strength of the Xiongnu army numbering tens of thousands, and fought many battles over a distance of a thousand *li*. Even when his army's path was blocked and their arrows gone, he had them brandish their longbows at the enemy and use their swords to fight to the death. He had so won the hearts of his followers that they were willing to do this. Not even the most famous generals of the past could have surpassed him in this. Though his army was defeated, their valiant effort was worthy of celebration throughout the empire. And it seemed to him, this official went on, that in not dying but becoming a prisoner, Li Ling's aim must have been to serve the Han secretly in some way, in that enemy land....

The assembled courtiers were stunned. It was unthinkable that anyone would dare to speak like this. They looked up in fear at the face of Emperor Wu, the veins on whose temples seemed about to burst. Then they thought of what fate awaited this man who had called them "courtiers whose only wish was to preserve themselves and safeguard their wives and children," and they smiled.

No sooner had this audacious man, Sima Qian, the Grand Historian, left the emperor's presence than one of these "courtiers whose only wish was to preserve themselves and safeguard their wives and children" spoke to Emperor Wu about the alleged friendship between Qian and Li Ling. Another claimed that the Grand Historian's statements were a reflection of a rift between Qian and General Li Guangli, saying that Qian's praise for Ling was intended to disgrace General Li, who had left the fort before Ling arrived but had accomplished nothing. At any rate, everyone joined in the view that Qian's attitude was far too high and mighty for a mere Grand Historian, whose job was to serve as astrologer, calendar-maker, and declarer of auspicious and inauspicious days.

Strange to say, Sima Qian was punished even before Li Ling's own family. The following day, he was put into the custody of the head of the Board of Punishments, the appointed penalty being castration.

In China from ancient times there were four principal types of punitive mutilation: tattooing, cutting off the nose, cutting off the feet, and castration. During the reign of Emperor Wu's grandfather, Emperor Wen, three of the four were abolished, leaving only castration, that peculiar penalty by which a man is deprived of his manliness. It was sometimes called "the punishment of rottenness," perhaps because the resulting wound gave off a rotting odor, or perhaps because the man was thought to become like a rotten tree that cannot bear fruit. Those who had been punished in this way were known as "eunuchs," and most of the officials who served in the women's quarters of the palace were of course eunuchs. But that Sima Qian, of all men, should suffer such a punishment!

Still, though we of later ages know him as the famous author of the *Historical Records*, we must remember that, at the time, Sima Qian was an insignificant official in charge of writings at court. His was unquestionably a brilliant intellect, but he had too much confidence in his abilities, was hard to get along with, never lost in debate with others, and was known to his contemporaries merely as a stubborn eccentric. No one was terribly surprised that he had met with "the punishment of rottenness."

The Sima clan had originally been court historians in the state of Zhou. Later they went to Jin and then served at the Chin court; and Sima Tan, in the fourth generation during the Han dynasty, served Emperor Wu and became Grand Historian in the Qianyuan era (140–135 BCE). Tan was Qian's father. Apart from law, calendar-making, and divination according to the *Yijing*, which were his professional specialties, he was well versed in the teachings of Daoism and familiar also with the doctrines of the various schools—Confucian, Mohist, Legalist, and Nominalist. He mastered all of these views and synthesized them into a system of his own.

His strong confidence in his own intellect and spiritual powers was passed on intact to his son Qian. But Tan's greatest educational gift to his son was sending him on a grand tour of the empire upon the completion of his studies. This was not a common way of finishing an education in those days, but it goes without saying that this grand tour played a very major role in making Sima Qian the historian that he later became.

When in 110 BCE Emperor Wu climbed Mount Tai in the east and worshipped Heaven, the hot-tempered Sima Tan, who happened to be lying ill in Zhounan at the time, was grieved that he alone was unable to accompany the emperor on this auspicious occasion of building the Han's first ritual mound. The indignity of this was so overwhelming that he died. It had been his most cherished desire in life to compile a comprehensive history from ancient to contemporary times, but he had only gotten as far as the collection of materials.

The scene of Tan's death is depicted in detail by his son Qian in the final chapter of the *Historical Records*. We are told that as soon as Sima Tan realized that he would not recover, he summoned Qian and, taking his hand, spoke earnestly of the necessity of writing history. He wept as he lamented the fact that he, the Grand Historian, had failed to accomplish this and was guilty of allowing the accomplishments of wise rulers and loyal ministers to be buried in the dust. "When I die, you will surely become Grand Historian. When that happens, do not forget what I sought to write!" When he said that this would be Qian's highest act of filial piety, the son bowed his head, weeping, and vowed that he would not disobey his father.

Two years after his father died, Sima Qian did indeed succeed to the post of Grand Historian. He immediately set his hand to the vocation that his father had bequeathed him, using the materials Tan had collected as well as secret documents stored in the palace. His first official duty after being appointed, however, was the major task of calendar revision, which required a full four years of his attention. When in 104 BCE it was done, he set to work at once on the writing of the *Historical Records*. Qian was at the time forty-two years of age.

He already knew what he wanted to achieve: a work of history that would be unlike any that had come before it. He approved of the *Spring and Autumn Annals* for its providing standards of moral and ethical criticism, but found its factual side wanting. More facts were what was wanted—not moral lessons, but facts. The *Commentary of Master Zuo and the Accounts of the States* contained an abundance of facts, to be sure. One could only marvel at the narrative skills of Master Zuo, but he did not explore the nature of the individual actors who created the facts he related. Zuo's descriptions were vivid, but there was no investigation of character or motive: this seemed highly unsatisfactory to Sima Qian.

In addition, all previous histories aimed at giving an account of the past to present-day readers and seemed little interested in relating present-day affairs to readers in the future. In short, Sima Qian could not find what he sought in existing works of history. As for what precisely was unsatisfactory about those histories—Qian felt that he would come to a clear understanding of that only when he had tried his own hand at writing what he wished. Yet it was not so much criticism of existing histories that motivated him as a need to express the vague notions pent up within himself.

Indeed, his criticism of other histories simply took the form of creating something new of his own. He was not even sure whether the concepts that he had limned in his mind for so long could in fact be called "history." But whether or not that was the case, he had not the shadow of a doubt that it needed to be written—for the sake of the people of his age and of later ages and, above all, for his own sake.

As was the case with Confucius, Sima Qian's policy was "to relate and not create," but his relating and not creating were rather different from the Sage's. For Sima Qian the mere listing of events in chronological order did not constitute "relating," while moralizing judgments that would impede future generations from knowing the facts themselves struck him as falling into the category of "creating."

Five successive reigns totaling one hundred years had elapsed since the founding of the Han dynasty, and books that had been destroyed or hidden due to the anti-cultural policies of the First Emperor of the Qin began to reappear at last. The literary arts seemed on the point of flourishing once again. It was not only the Han court but the times themselves that demanded the writing of histories. For Sima Qian, the deep emotions aroused by his father's final injunction were conjoined to broad learning, powers of observation, and literary skill; and all these had matured to a point where the writing of a nearly perfect history could be achieved. His work went well—almost too well, to his way of thinking. From the chronicles of the first five emperors of China down to the Xia, Yin, Zhou, and Qin dynasties, he was little more than a technician arranging materials in the service of strict narrative accuracy. But when he passed from the reign of the First Emperor of the Qin and began to chronicle the life of General Xiang Yu at the beginning of the Han dynasty—including his fatal troubles with the founder of the Han after Xiang Yu became a "king," or local ruler, Qian began to be unsure about how cool and neutral a technician he could continue to be. It might happen, somehow, that Xiang Yu would take possession of him, or he of Xiang Yu.

> King Xiang then rose in the night and was drinking behind the curtains of his tent. A beautiful woman was with him. Her name was Yu. She was so much favored by the king that she always attended him. He had a fine steed whose name was Zhui, which he always used to ride. Thereupon King Xiang improvised a

poem expressing his sorrow and anger: "My power can penetrate mountains and my spirit cover the world, yet the times are not propitious, and Zhui will not go forward. What can I do if he refuses to go forward? And what shall I do about thee, my Yu, my Yu?" He sang a few verses, and the beautiful Yu joined in the song. King Xiang shed tears. Those around him all wept, and none could look upon him.

Sima Qian wondered if this kind of writing was appropriate. Could he allow himself to write so passionately about past events? He wanted to be wary of "creating." His job was only "to relate." In fact, all he had done was to relate events. But with what vividness he related them! His kind of narration would be quite impossible for someone without an extraordinarily imaginative visual sense. Sometimes, out of an excess of fear that he was "creating," he would reread a passage he had written and cut the phrases that made historical figures seem to behave as if they were actual living persons. Then the vital breath would vanish from those figures, and there would be no need to worry about his having "created" them. But, it seemed to Sima Qian, at this point Xiang Yu ceased to be Xiang Yu. Xiang Yu and the First Emperor of the Qin and King Zhuang of Qu all became the same kind of person. How could depicting very different people as if they were the same be called "relating"?

Also, "to relate" was to depict different people as different, was it not? Looking at things in this way, he could not help but restore the phrases he had earlier deleted. He would put them back in, try reading the passage once again, and finally be content. And not only he: the historical figures depicted—Xiang Yu, Fan Kuai, Fan Zeng—all seemed at last to calm down and settle into their place in history.

When in good spirits, Emperor Wu was a truly wise, magnanimous, and understanding protector of letters and learning. Moreover, since the position of Grand Historian was one that required an unspectacular but very special kind of skill, Sima Qian was able to avoid the insecurity with regard to one's position (or one's very life) as a result of the slander and detraction from colleagues that was almost inevitable in official life.

For some years, then, Sima Qian led a full and happy life. (The happiness envisioned by the men of that period was a very different thing from our present conceptions, but the quest for happiness was the same.) He was not one to compromise; but he was positive and active, often debating, often indignant, often amused; and his favorite occupation was beating his opponents in argument to the point where they had not a leg left to stand on.

And then, after some years of such a life, this calamity descended upon him.

The light was dim inside the "silkworm chamber." It was necessary to avoid all exposure to the wind for some time after a castration was performed, so a dark, tightly sealed room was built, and a fire kept going for warmth; and there the castrated prisoner was kept to enable him to recover. Since the warm, dark room was similar to the chamber in which silkworms were raised, it was so named.

Disturbed beyond words, Sima Qian leaned vacantly against a wall. He was not so much angry as thunderstruck. He had always been ready to face death by beheading, for example. He could imagine himself being executed; and he had had forebodings of that when he spoke up in defense of Li Ling, risking the emperor's anger. But that he should be subjected to castration, the most shameful of all punishments! He had, no doubt, been too heedless (for if one is prepared for death, one must be prepared for any punishment); but he had never considered the possibility of such an ugly fate as this. He had always believed that, in this life, only things appropriate to a person happened—an idea that had come to him from his long study of history. Thus, in adverse circumstances, a gentleman who is righteously indignant over the state of the nation will experience intense, violent pain, while a weaker man will have to endure a slow, gloomy, ugly pain. Even if what happens to a man seems at first sight unjust, his response to his situation will ultimately demonstrate that his fate well suits him.

Sima Qian believed himself to be a manly person. True, he was a writer; but he felt sure that he was more of a man than any of the military men of his day. And it was not only he who thought so: even those who had not the least liking for him could not but acknowledge that fact. Thus, he could imagine himself—if he insisted on his personal views—facing execution by being tied to two carriages and torn apart. But to face a humiliating punishment like this when he was almost fifty years of age! That he should now be in this "silkworm chamber" seemed like a nightmare. He wanted it to be a bad dream. But then, leaning against the wall and opening his eyes, he saw in the dimness three or four men sitting or lying every which way, their faces lifeless, as if their very souls had left them. When he realized that he was in that same condition, a cry burst from him, a cry that was something between a sob and a bellow.

During the several days of anger and pain that followed, thoughts came to him, the result of ingrained habits of scholarly reflection: What, in fact, had gone wrong? Who had done what to cause all this? He first blamed Emperor Wu (the Way of Lord and Subject in China being fundamentally different from that in Japan). Indeed, his resentment against his sovereign was for a time so intense as to make him forget everything else. When, however, this brief period of violent feeling had passed, the historian within him was reawakened. Unlike the orthodox Confucianists, he knew how necessary it was, as a historian, to discount the inflated reputations of the sagely Previous Kings, as they were termed; and so he could not now allow personal resentment to distort his historical evaluation of Emperor Wu, a Latter-day King.

Emperor Wu was undeniably a great ruler. Despite his various defects, so long as he was sovereign, the empire of the Han was unshakable. Leaving aside for the moment the merits of the Founding Emperor of the dynasty, one had to admit that both Emperor Wen, "the Benevolent," and Emperor Jing, "the Illustrious," were minor figures compared to Emperor Wu. But the defects of major figures are also major—that is the way of the world—and it was incumbent on Sima Qian not to forget that, even in the midst of his intense anger. One had to regard what had happened as an act of Heaven, on a par with plagues, typhoons, and violent thunderstorms.

Thus, reflection would push him now toward even more despairing indignation and now toward a kind of resignation. Finding that he could not forever direct his fierce resentment toward the sovereign, inevitably he aimed it at the wicked ministers surrounding the ruler. They were wicked, no doubt about it; but theirs was a very minor kind of wickedness. Besides, Sima Qian had so high a sense of self-respect that he could not find satisfaction in taking such petty persons as objects of his resentment.

But never before had he felt such anger at apparently "good-natured" people. They were harder to deal with than the obviously wicked ministers and cruel officials. Observing their doings infuriated Sima Qian. They enjoyed a cheap, "conscientious" peace of mind and helped others to enjoy it, too, and it was this that made their behavior all the more shameful. They would neither defend nor confute. Inwardly, there was neither self-examination nor self-reproach.

Prime Minister Gongsun He was a prime example of this type. When it came to toadying to the powerful, a man like Du Zhou (who had recently brought down Wang Ching and cleverly managed to take his place as Superintendent of the Impeachment Court) knew exactly what he was doing; but this fool of a prime minister was not even aware of what he himself did. Even were he to be called "the kind of minister who seeks only to save himself and protect his wife and children," it would not anger this fellow in the least. Finally, he too was not worth directing one's resentment against.

At last Sima Qian began to direct his rage at himself. If he had to be angry at someone, there could be no better object than himself. But where had he gone wrong? He could not possibly regard his defense of Li Ling as a mistake; nor did he feel his choice of methods was particularly bad. Speaking out was the only thing he could have done if he did not wish to descend to the level of a sycophant. If, looking back, he found nothing to be ashamed of, a gentleman worthy of the name ought to accept whatever resulted from acting honorably. That could not be denied. Therefore he was prepared to accept his punishment, even if it meant amputation of his limbs or being cut in half at the waist.

But castration—and the physical state resulting from that punishment—that was another matter entirely. It was different from losing a foot or a nose to the executioner. It was not a punishment to be inflicted upon a gentleman. Indeed, this bodily condition he was left with was, viewed from whatever angle, a perfect evil. It could not be disguised with fine words. A wound to the spirit might heal with time, but the hideous reality of his body would be with him until death. Whatever his motives might have been, anything that invited such a result had to be termed wrong. But what, precisely, had been wrong? What wrong had he done? None whatsoever. He had done nothing but what was right. Perhaps it was the mere fact of his existence that was at fault.

Sima Qian would be sitting in the "silkworm chamber" in a vague, absent state, and then suddenly jump up and begin pacing around the warm, dim room, moaning like a wounded animal. He kept repeating these actions unconsciously, and his thoughts, too, went round and round the same point, never coming to a conclusion.

Several times he found himself butting his head against the wall until his blood flowed, but apart from that, he never attempted to harm himself. He wanted to die—how good it would be if he could! He had no fear of death because a sense of shame that was far more fearsome relentlessly pursued him. Why, then, could he not die? Partly because he had none of the tools needed for suicide in this prison. There was, however, something else that stopped him from committing suicide, something from inside himself. At first, he was not aware of what it was. Although he often felt a fitful urge to die in the midst of his frenzy and resentment, he was also vaguely aware of something that would not let his emotions move in the direction of suicide.

It sometimes happens that one feels as if one has forgotten something but cannot say quite what. That was Sima Qian's situation. It was only after he had been permitted to return to his residence, under strict orders to refrain from leaving it, that he realized that he had, during the madness of the past month, forgotten about his life's work, the compilation and writing of the history. He realized too that, although he had forgotten about it on one level, his unconscious commitment to that work had played a role in keeping him from suicide.

His father's agonized words as he lay on his deathbed ten years before, weeping as he took his son's hand, still resounded in his ears. But it was not those words alone that kept him from giving up his work on the history, even in his present harrowing state of mind. It was, above all, the work itself. Not the charm of the work, or his enthusiasm for it—not something so pleasant as that. He realized, of course, that it was his mission to write the history, but this realization was not born of proud self-reliance. He had been a very egotistical man, but what had happened made him painfully aware of how worthless he really was. He had been proud of his ideals and aspirations, but in fact he amounted to no more than a worm crushed under the hooves of cattle by the roadside.

Yes, his ego had been crushed, but there could be no doubt about the value of his work as a historian. Having lost all self-confidence, all self-reliance, having been reduced to this contemptible state, he would nonetheless live on in this world and accomplish his task—not that he would take any pleasure in it. It felt to him like the kind of human relationship that seems destined, fated, and that one cannot, finally, break off, no matter how repugnant it may be. It was absolutely clear to him that, as long as he had this work to do, he could never kill himself. This was not from a mere sense of duty, but due to an almost physical bond with the work.

Now, in place of the blind, animal suffering he had first experienced after his castration, there was a more conscious, human suffering. Unfortunately, with the clear realization that he could not commit suicide came a steadily clearer realization that there was no other means of escape from his suffering and shame, apart from suicide. The strong and healthy Grand Historian Sima Qian died in the spring of Tianhan 3; and the Sima Qian who later continued the unfinished history was no more than a writing-machine, without intelligence or consciousness. It was essential for Sima Qian to convince himself of this, and so he tried his best to do so. The writing of the history *must* be carried on. For him, this was an absolute. For the work to be carried on, he had to continue to live, no matter how hard it was to endure. In order to continue to live, he had to convince himself that his person no longer existed.

After the fifth lunar month had passed, Sima Qian once again took up his writing-brush. There was neither joy nor excitement in this: He was just whipped on by his will to complete the work; and so, like a traveler dragging himself on sore, injured legs toward his destination, he plodded on with the manuscript. He had been relieved of his post as Grand Historian, but Emperor Wu, a little regretful of what he had done, made Sima Qian head of the Department of Documents. To Qian, however, official advancement or degradation no longer had any meaning. He who had been such a keen debater now never opened his mouth, and neither laughed nor showed anger.

Yet he did not appear despondent or dispirited. On the contrary, people saw in his silent visage a terrifying quality, as if he were possessed by an evil spirit. He carried on with his work, even begrudging the time he had to spend in sleep at night. He seemed to his family to be in a great hurry to finish the work as quickly as possible so he would then be free to take his own life.

After applying himself grimly for a year or so, Sima Qian discovered at last that, even after having lost all joy in living, there was still joy to be found in self-expresssion. Even then, however, he maintained his perfect silence, and the terrifying harshness of his countenance remained unsoftened. When, in the course of writing the history, he came to passages where he had to use the words "eunuch" or "gelding," he could not suppress a groan. Whether he was alone in his study or lying on his bed at night, whenever the memory of his humiliation came back to him, a throbbing pain would run through his body, as if he had been burned with a hot iron. He would jump up, letting out a strange cry, and begin to walk about the room for a time, moaning. Then, gnashing his teeth, he would endeavor to compose himself.

Three

Li Ling had lost consciousness in the thick of battle, and he awakened to find himself in the khan's tent, lit by animal-fat lamps and warmed by a fire made with dried dung. He understood his situation immediately. He had only two choices: To cut his own throat and so escape the shame of captivity, or to yield to his captors for the time being while waiting for a chance to make his escape—and take back with him a trophy sufficient to atone for his defeat in battle. It was this second course that Li Ling decided upon.

The Xiongnu khan released Li Ling from his bonds with his own hands, and his treatment of his captive thereafter was exceedingly courteous. Judihou Khan, the younger brother of his predecessor, Goulihu Khan, was a sturdily built middle-aged warrior, goggle-eyed and with a reddish beard. Like several generations of Xiongnu leaders before him, he had fought against the Han; but he frankly admitted that he had never come up against an opponent as tough as Li Ling, praising his military skills as comparable to those of Li Ling's grandfather, Li Guang. The illustrious name of Li Guang, "the Flying General," who had killed a tiger with his bare hands and pierced a large rock with an arrow, was talked of even now, and even in barbarian lands. The cordial treatment that Ling received was due to his being the grandson of a man of such strength, and to his own as well. It was the Xiongnu custom when dividing up food, for example, for the strong to take the tastiest parts, leaving the remainder for the old and weak. Among the Xiongnu, it was out of the question to humiliate a powerful man. Thus, the captive general Li Ling was given his own tent with several dozen attendants and treated with all the courtesy due to an honored guest.

And so there began what was for Li Ling a strange new way of life. His dwelling was a curtained and carpeted tent; his food, mutton; and his drink, the milk of sheep and cows, and fermented koumiss. For clothing, there were furs and the hides of wolves, bears, and sheep sewn together.

Herding, hunting, and pillaging were the whole of life for the Xiongnu. Yet even on the apparently limitless high plain, there were borders formed by rivers, lakes, and mountains. Apart from the land under the direct rule of the khan were the territories of various Xiongnu nobles, beginning with the lords Zuoxian, Yuxian, Zuoluli, and Yululi; and the migrations of the nomads were confined to each area. It was a land without towns and without fields. Even the villages that did exist shifted location from season to season in pursuit of grass and water.

Li Ling was not given any land. He always accompanied the khan, together with the Xiongnu commanders who served directly under their ruler. If the opportunity presented itself, Ling would have liked to take the khan's head; but such a chance was unlikely to come. Even had he managed to kill the khan, it would have been impossible to escape with the head as trophy, barring exceptionally good luck. If he succeeded in killing the khan but were himself killed in the barbarians' territory, the Xiongnu would be sure to hush up the whole matter as bringing dishonor to themselves; so word of Li Ling's deed would never get back to the Han. Nonetheless, Li Ling patiently awaited the arrival of that virtually impossible opportunity.

There were several other Han captives in the khan's encampment. One of them, Wei Lu, was not a military man but was treated with the greatest regard by the khan, having been given the rank of Lord Dingling. His father had been a Xiongnu, but Wei Lu happened to be born and raised in the Han capital. He had served under Emperor Wu, but fearing he would be implicated in the affair of Master of Music Li Yan-nian some years before, he fled to the barbarians' territory and joined the Xiongnu. Blood tells, after all, and he was able quickly to accustom himself to the barbarians' ways. He was also a very able man and always attended Judihou Khan's war council, being party to all plans and discussions. Li Ling hardly ever spoke with Wei Lu or other Han who were now among the Xiongnu. He was sure none among them would choose to become a partner in the plans he was quietly forming. And in fact all the Han captives in the camp seemed to feel uncomfortable with each other and never formed close friendships.

It happened that the khan summoned Li Ling, asking him for instruction on a point of military strategy. Since it was part of a war with the Eastern Hu, another barbarian state, Ling readily gave his advice. The next time the khan consulted him, it had to do with strategy against the Han army. Li Ling showed his displeasure by the look on his face, saying not a word; and the khan did not press the matter. Some time after this, Ling was asked to go south as one of the commanders of an army aiming to raid two districts in northern China. This time Li Ling flatly refused, saying that he could not participate in action against Han. Thereafter, the khan never again made such a request. His treatment of Li Ling was unchanged. It seemed that he had no ulterior motive: He wished to accord gentlemanly treatment to his prisoner because he recognized him as a gentleman. Li Ling, for his part, felt that the khan was, in the true sense, a man.

The khan's eldest son, Lord Zuoxian, started to show unusual goodwill toward Li Ling—or rather, respect for him. He had just turned twenty—and was a bit coarse, but a brave and serious youth. His regard for strength was intense and pure. When he first visited Li Ling, he asked the general to tutor him in mounted archery. The mounted part presented no problem: he was easily a match for Li Ling on horseback. Indeed, he far surpassed the older man when it came to riding without a saddle. Li Ling therefore decided to focus on archery, and Lord Zuoxian became his devoted student. When Ling told him about his grandfather Li Guang's almost superhuman skill in archery, the barbarian youth listened eagerly, his eyes shining.

The two often hunted together. With only a few attendants, they would race over the plains, hunting foxes, wolves, antelope, eagles, and pheasants. It once happened that, as dusk fell, they had used up all their arrows, and their horses having far outpaced those of their attendants, they found themselves surrounded by a pack of wolves. Whipping their horses on, they broke through the pack at full speed. A wolf leapt onto the rump of Li Ling's horse, but young Lord Zuoxian, who had been riding just behind, slashed through the wolf's body with a single stroke of his scimitar. A quick look revealed that the legs of both of their horses had been bitten and torn at by the wolves and were covered with blood. After a day like this, as they sat in their tent at night blowing on the hot broth made from their catch before drinking it down, Li Ling suddenly felt something akin to friendship for this young barbarian prince, his cheeks rosy in the firelight.

In the autumn of Tianhan 3, the Xiongnu again attacked Yanmen in north China. In retaliation, in Tianhan 4, the Han had General Li Guangli leave Shuofang at the head of an army of sixty thousand cavalry and seventy thousand foot-soldiers. Commander of Crossbow Troops Lu Bode was sent to assist him with ten thousand men. Soon after, General Gong Sun'ao advanced from Yanmen with ten thousand cavalry and thirty thousand infantry, while General Han Yue advanced from Wuyuan with thirty thousand foot-soldiers.

This northern campaign was on a scale unprecedented in recent years. As soon as the khan learned of it, he ordered that the women, the very old and very young, and his herds and valuables be transferred to an area north of the Shewu River. Then, leading one hundred thousand of his best cavalry, he attacked the forces of Li Guangli and Lu Bode on the great plain south of the river. The battle went on for more than ten days. Finally the Han army was forced to withdraw.

Young Lord Zuoxian, who had studied under Li Ling, was in command of his own battalion, which moved east to confront General Gong Sun'ao and destroyed him utterly. General Han Yue's forces, constituting the left flank of the Han army, likewise failed to win the day, and withdrew. The northern campaign had been a total failure.

As usual, Li Ling never appeared in the Xiongnu camp while battle with the Han forces was ongoing, keeping to the north of the river. But he was shocked to find himself privately anxious about how well Lord Zuoxian was doing. Of course he hoped, on the whole, for a Han victory and a Xiongnu defeat. Yet he seemed to feel that Lord Zuoxian, at least, must not be allowed to lose. When he became aware of this feeling, Li Ling censured himself severely.

Gong Sun'ao, who had been defeated by Lord Zuoxian, returned to the capital, and when imprisoned on charges of having lost numerous troops without achieving anything, he offered a peculiar defense. An enemy prisoner, he claimed, had said that the Xiongnu army was so strong because General Li, who had surrendered to the nomads, was training the troops and preparing the Xiongnu for war against the Han forces by teaching them military strategy. Now this in itself was not an adequate defense against the charge of having been defeated, so General Gong was not pardoned; but it goes without saying that Emperor Wu, hearing this, was filled with fury against Li Ling. Ling's family members, who had been pardoned and allowed to return home, were

once again imprisoned; and this time everyone, from his elderly mother
to his wife, children, and younger brothers, was executed. In the way
typical of shallow people, the gentry and officials of Longxi, the Li family's hometown, were filled with shame that their town had produced
such a family, the records tell us.

It took about a half year for the news of all this to reach Li Ling.
When he first heard it, from the mouth of a Han soldier who had been
abducted from a frontier area, Li Ling leapt to his feet, grabbed the prisoner by the collar and shook him roughly, trying to learn whether he
was telling the truth. When he determined that the man was not lying,
Ling gritted his teeth and tightened his grip. The prisoner struggled and
let out an agonized groan. Without knowing what he was doing, Ling
had choked the breath out of him. When he released his grip, the man
fell to the ground. Without giving him a second glance, Ling rushed
from the tent.

He walked over the grassland in a terrible state. A fierce anger
swirled inside him. When he thought of his aged mother and his young
children, his heart burned within him yet he shed not a single tear. Anger so intense must have the effect of drying up all one's tears.

It was not only this time. What kind of treatment had his family
received from Han over the years? He thought of the way his grandfather Li Guang had died. (Ling's father Danghu had died a few months
prior to his birth, making Ling a "posthumous child." It was his famous
grandfather, therefore, who educated and trained him in his boyhood.)
The renowned General Li Guang had made great contributions on numerous northern campaigns yet had never received any reward, due to
the machinations of the evil sycophants surrounding the throne. Various commanders who were his subordinates went on to be ennobled
and enfeoffed, but the honest and upright general, far from being en-
riched, had to endure poverty to the end of his days. Finally Li Guang
had a run-in with Generalissimo Wei Qing. Wei Qing himself felt sympathy for the aged General Li, but one of the officials serving under him,
wrongly borrowing his authority, humiliated Li Guang. The famous old
general, infuriated, cut his own throat on the spot, in the midst of the
army camp. Even now Ling could clearly remember himself as a boy

hearing the news of his grandfather's death, and wailing....

And what about the death of Ling's uncle Li Gan, who was Li Guang's second son? Filled with resentment against Wei Qing because of his father's miserable death, he went to the Generalissimo's residence and berated him publicly. General Huo Qubing, the Generalissimo's nephew, was indignant at this, and used the occasion of a hunt at the Sweet Springs Palace to shoot Li Gan with a fatal arrow. Emperor Wu knew what had happened, but, wishing to protect General Huo, had it announced that Li Gan had died as a result of a wound from a deer's antler....

Li Ling's feelings were far less mixed than Sima Qian's. They could be summed up in the word "outrage." (Apart, that is, from the remorseful thought: "If only I had managed to act sooner and carry out my original plan, escaping from the Xiongnu lands with the khan's head in hand....") The only question was how to express this outrage. He recalled the words of the soldier he had questioned, that the Emperor was infuriated to learn that General Li was instructing the barbarian soldiers and preparing them to fight against the Han. And then he understood: He himself had, of course, never done such a thing; but there was another captive Han general in Xiongnu hands, named Li Xu. He had originally been a Commander-Beyond-the-Great-Wall, charged with protecting Xihoucheng; but after his capture, he had regularly instructed the Xiongnu army on military strategy and trained the troops. Indeed, he had followed the khan into battle against the Han forces as recently as a half year before. This was the General Li who was meant, and for whom Li Ling had been mistaken at the Han Court.

That evening he went alone to Li Xu's tent. He said not a word, and allowed the other to say nothing. One stroke of the sword, and Li Xu fell dead.

The next morning Li Ling went before the khan and confessed what he had done. The khan told him there was no need to worry, although the queen mother might create difficulties. The khan's mother, despite her advanced years, was involved in a licentious relationship with Li Xu, which the khan had accepted. According to Xiongnu custom, when a father died, his eldest son took all of the late man's wives and concubines and made them his own. His own birth-mother was the single exception—respect for one's mother being maintained even among this people, among whom women in general were held in such low esteem.

The khan urged Li Ling to go into hiding in the north for a time, adding that he would send a messenger for him when the storm blew over. Following this advice, Li Ling went into hiding in the foothills of Elindaban Peak to the northwest, along with several attendants.

Soon after, the difficult queen mother took ill and died. Summoned to return to the khan's court, Li Ling seemed a different person. Up to then, he had absolutely refused to take part in any strategies aimed against the Han, but now he himself said he would gladly offer his advice. The khan rejoiced to see this change. He named his captive general Lord Youxiao, the Commander of the Royal Guard, and gave him one of his own daughters in marriage. There had earlier been talk of such a marriage, but Ling had always refused. Now, however, he accepted the khan's gift without hesitation.

A Xiongnu force was just about to move south to attack and pillage the area around Jiuquan and Zhangye, and Ling asked to be allowed to go along. But when their route to the southwest happened to pass through the foothills of Mount Xunji, his spirits fell. He remembered the men under his command who had fought to the death on this spot. As he walked over the sand where their bones were buried and which their blood had once stained, and thought of his own present condition, he lost the heart to continue southward and fight against the Han. Claiming illness, he rode back to the north, alone.

The next year, Tai Shi 1, according to the Chinese calendar, Judihou Khan died and was succeeded by Lord Zuoxian, who was on such close terms with Li Ling. He assumed the title Hulugu Khan.

Li Ling had become Lord Youxiao of the Xiongnu, but his mind was still unsettled. Though he felt in every fiber of his being a burning resentment at the extermination of his mother, wife, and children, yet it was clear from his recent experience that he could not bring himself to lead troops to fight against the Han. He had vowed never to set foot on Han territory again; but, despite his close friendship with the new khan, he was by no means sure that he could be content to live totally according to Xiongnu ways and to end his life among them. He did not much like thinking, and so, when he was upset, he would mount a swift horse and gallop over the plains alone. He would ride like a madman over grasslands and hilly ground, his horse's hooves clattering under the clear blue skies of autumn. After racing for several dozen li, both horse and rider would tire, and Ling would look for a brook flowing through the plateau, where he would dismount and water his horse.

Then he would lie on his back on the grass and gaze up, with a pleasurable sense of fatigue, at the blue sky in all its clarity, height, and breadth. At times he would suddenly feel himself to be a mere speck between earth and sky, and wonder why in heaven's name there were such distinctions as Han and Hun. After a good rest, he would again mount his horse and begin to gallop wildly over the plain. Fatigued from his day's ride, he would return to camp as yellow clouds of dust darkened the setting sun. Exhaustion was his only salvation.

He had heard that Sima Qian had been found guilty of speaking in his defense. Li Ling felt neither special gratitude for this nor pity. He knew Sima Qian slightly and had exchanged greetings with him, but they had never established a relationship. Indeed, Ling had thought Qian a rather troublesome man, overly fond of disputation. Besides, Ling was far too caught up in the struggle with his own pain to have much sympathy for the misfortunes of others. He may not have gone so far as to think that Sima Qian should have minded his own business, but it was a fact that he did not feel particularly grateful either.

The nomads' customs, which had at first seemed coarse and grotesque, were, when viewed against the backdrop of the actual geography and climate of the land, by no means either vulgar or irrational, Li Ling gradually came to see. Without wearing clothing made of thick animal hides, one could not endure the northern winters; without eating meat, one could not store enough energy to endure the intense cold of the region. Their way of life decreed that they not build fixed dwellings:

that too could not be simply dismissed as "low-class." If one were to try to conform to the ways of the Han in everything, one could not survive even for one day in the midst of that natural environment.

Li Ling recalled the words of the former khan, Judihou, criticizing the Han for constantly praising their own nation as "the land of good manners," while regarding the ways of the Xiongnu as akin to those of animals. "What are these 'good manners' that the Han talk of? Doesn't it mean an empty show? Hiding what is ugly under a veneer of beautiful ornamentation? When it comes to loving self-advantage and envying others, who is worse, the Han or the Xiongnu? And as to lust and greed, which side is worse? Tear off the veneer, and there is finally no difference between the two! The only difference is that the men of Han know how to cover it up, while we do not."

When the khan went on to give specific examples of internecine fighting and the exclusion and overthrow of worthy ministers throughout the Han dynasty, Li Ling was hard pressed to make any reply. He himself, as a military man, had often felt doubts about the burdensome "manners for the sake of manners" that prevailed at the Han Court. Certainly the rough directness of the Xiongnu often seemed far preferable to the craftiness of the Han, hiding itself behind fine words. To take it for granted that Chinese customs were right and nomadic customs base—was that not merely a biased view on the part of the Han? Over time, it came to seem so to Li Ling. For instance, he had always assumed that a person needed to have a "social name" in addition to his "personal name"; but when you considered the matter, there was no reason why one absolutely had to have a separate name for use in society.

His new Xiongnu wife was a very gentle woman. She remained timid and apprehensive in front of her husband, and hardly spoke. But the son who was born to them was not the least bit afraid of his father and would climb up on to his lap to be held. As he gazed into the child's face, memories of his other children—those whom he had left behind in Chang'an, and who had been killed along with their mother and grandmother—would suddenly come to mind, and Li Ling would, despite himself, feel dejected.

Exactly one year before Li Ling went over to the Xiongnu, Su Wu, Commander of the Han Palace Guards, was detained in nomad territory. Su Wu had originally been dispatched as a peace envoy to arrange an exchange of prisoners. His vice envoy, however, had become involved in an internal struggle among the Xiongnu; as a result, Su Wu's entire party was taken prisoner. The khan did not wish to kill them, but rather to force them to go over to their captors by using the threat of death.

Su Wu alone would not agree to surrender and actually stabbed himself in the chest with a sword in an attempt to avoid the shame of captivity. The nomad doctor charged with treating the Han envoy, who had lost consciousness, employed a very unusual method of treatment. According to the *History of the Han*, he had a hole dug and embers buried at the bottom, then laid the wounded man down on the earth above the buried embers and stepped on his back until Su Wu's blood began to flow. Thanks to this harsh course of treatment, Su Wu, to his great sorrow, revived after having been unconscious for a half day.

Judihou Khan regarded Su Wu with great favor. When, after several weeks, Su Wu had fully recovered physically, the khan sent his advisor Wei Lu to urge most strongly once again that the Han envoy submit to the Xiongnu. Wei Lu's efforts were met with a hail of fiery words from Su Wu, and he withdrew, thoroughly shamed. After that, Su Wu was confined in a pit, where he escaped starvation by eating wool fluff mixed with snow. Finally he was moved to an unpopulated place on the banks of Lake Baikal and told that he would be allowed to return to his country "when rams gave milk."

Because these events are so well known, together with Su Wu's fame as one who remained faithful to his duty for nineteen long years, they will not be recounted in detail here. At any rate, around the time that Li Ling was at last forced to decide to bury himself in the nomad lands for the painful remnants of his days, a solitary Su Wu had been tending sheep for many years on the shores of Lake Baikal, "the Northern Sea."

Su Wu had been Li Ling's friend for twenty years. They had served as advisers to Emperor Wu around the same time. Ling knew that, although Su Wu had an obdurate, unsociable side, he was without question a man of rare character and conviction. When, in Tianhan 1, shortly after Su Wu's departure for the north, his aged mother died of illness, Ling went with the funeral procession as far as the cemetery at Yangling. When Ling himself was about to leave for his northern campaign, he heard the news that Su Wu's wife, despairing of his return to Han, had gone off to become the wife of another man; thinking of his friend, Ling was highly indignant at the woman's inconstancy.

After he had unwillingly submitted to the Xiongnu, however, Li Ling no longer wanted to meet Su Wu. He was glad that Su Wu had been moved to the far north where he would not have to see him face to face. Particularly after his family had been slaughtered and he had lost all desire to return to Han, he wished all the more to avoid an encounter with this "Sheep-herder Envoy."

Several years after Hulugu Khan had succeeded his father, there were rumors that questioned whether Su Wu was alive at all. Calling to mind this unyielding Han envoy whom his father had never been able to persuade to submit, Hulugu Khan—aware that Ling and Wu had been friends—asked Li Ling to determine whether Su Wu was still alive. If so, Ling was to urge him once again to capitulate. So Ling had to set out for the north.

He followed the Guqie River northward to its confluence with the Zhiju River and then went northwest through a forested area. After several days' travel along riverbanks that were still snowy in places, he glimpsed beyond the forest and plain the blue waters of Lake Baikal. A guide of the Dingling tribe, who lived in the area, led Li Ling and his party to a crude log cabin. The inhabitant of the cabin, startled by the unusual sound of human voices, emerged with bow and arrow in hand. It took a while for Li Ling to discover the former Su Ziching (as Su Wu was also known), Master of the Imperial Stables, in the guise of a bear-like mountain man with a bushy beard, clothed entirely in animal hides. And it took even longer for Su Wu to recognize this high official dressed in Xiongnu clothing as Li Shaoqing (Ling's other name), the former Commander of Cavalry. Su Wu had not even heard that Ling was now serving the Xiongnu.

Strong emotion swept away in an instant whatever in Ling had made him avoid meeting Wu until this moment. At first, both men were at a loss for words.

Ling's attendants set up several yurts nearby, and the hitherto lonely spot at once became lively. The food and wine they had brought with them were promptly transferred to the cabin; and that night, sounds of laughter that had never been heard there startled the birds and other woodland creatures.

It was hard indeed for Li Ling to explain how he had come to be dressed in Xiongnu fashion, but he laid out the facts without any admixture of self-justification. The life that Su Wu calmly described having led for the past few years sounded truly miserable to Li Ling. Some years before, the Xiongnu Lord Yugan, while out hunting, had happened to pass by and, feeling sorry for Su Wu, had supplied him with food and clothing for three years. But after Lord Yugan's death, Su Wu had had to ward off starvation by digging out field mice from the frozen earth, he said. The rumors concerning his possible death were a distortion of something that had actually happened: The herds that he was tending had been driven off by bandits and were no more.

Ling told Su Wu of his mother's death, but he could not bring himself to tell him that his wife had abandoned their children and gone off to marry into another family.

Ling wondered why this man carried on with his life. Did he still hope to return to Han someday? From what Su Wu said, it seemed he no longer had any such hopes. If so, why was he willing to endure so wretched an existence? It was guaranteed that he would be exceptionally well treated if he offered his submission to the khan, but it was clear to Li Ling from the beginning that Su Wu was not the kind of man to do such a thing. What puzzled Li Ling was why Su Wu had not taken his own life. If Li Ling himself was unable to end his hopeless life with his own hand, it was because he had put down roots in this land and was bound by numerous ties of duty and affection. Besides, at this point his death would not be regarded as fulfilling his duty to the Han.

But Su Wu's case was different. He had no ties to this land. And in terms of his fidelity to the Han Court, it would make little difference whether he starved to death on this plain, having held on to his envoy's insignia to the bitter end, or whether he burned the insignia at once and then cut his own throat. Having stabbed himself in the chest immediately after being captured, it was unthinkable that he would now start to fear death. Li Ling recalled Su Wu's stubbornness when he was young—an obstinate stoicism that was almost comical. The khan was trying to fish Su Wu out of extreme adversity with the bait of glory. To take the bait, of course, or even to kill himself to escape his hardships, would be to give in to the khan—or to Fate, as symbolized by the khan. Was not that how Su Wu felt?

But the sight of Su Wu engaged in a test of wills with Fate did not seem comical or ludicrous to Li Ling. If it was stubbornness that enabled someone to scorn unimaginable difficulties, deprivations, intense cold, and isolation—and this for the long stretch of time until one's death—then this stubbornness was surely a grand and awe-inspiring thing. Li Ling was filled with admiration at seeing Su Wu's former stoicism, which had seemed a bit childish at times, mature into this great power of endurance. Moreover, this man had no expectations that his conduct would become known in the land of Han. He had no hopes that he would ever be welcomed again in Han; or, indeed, that Han, or even the Xiongnu khan, would be informed of his ongoing struggles with harsh adversity in this desolate place. He would certainly die alone, unobserved by anyone; and he was determined on his last day to die with the satisfaction of being able to look back and laugh at his fate to the very end. He did not care whether anyone knew what he had accomplished.

Now Li Ling had at one time planned to take the head of the previous khan; but he feared that even if he achieved his goal, he would not be able to escape from Xiongnu territory with the head, and that would mean that his deed had been in vain, and that the Han would never hear of it. Thus, in the end, he had failed to find an opportunity to act. Confronted with Su Wu, who felt no regret at being unknown to others, he felt he might break into a cold sweat.

The first surge of emotion having passed, after two or three days Li Ling began to feel an uncontrollable fixation developing within himself. No matter what they discussed, the troubling contrast between his past and Su Wu's kept making itself felt. Su Wu the righteous man and himself the traitor—it was not so clear a distinction as that; but in the face of Su Wu's sternness, tempered by long years of silence among woods and fields and waters, he could not help feeling that his own suffering up until then, which was the only possible defense for his behavior, was reduced to insignificance. Then too—or was he only imagining it?—as the days passed, he began to sense in Su Wu's attitude toward him something of the rich man's attitude toward the poor man—an awareness of superiority leading to a conscious effort to be generous to the other. He could not quite put his finger on it, but occasionally he could sense it. In the gaze of Su Wu, dressed in rags, there appeared at times a faint tinge of pity, and this was what Li Ling, Lord Youxiao, appareled in rich sable furs, feared more than anything else.

After ten days, Li Ling parted from his old friend and returned to the south, dejected. He had left behind ample supplies of food and clothing in Su Wu's log cabin in the forest. He had, in the end, not broached the subject of submission, despite the khan's charge to him to do so. Since it was unquestionably clear what Su Wu's answer would be, what would have been the point of shaming both Su Wu and himself by making such an appeal?

Even after Li Ling had returned south, the thought of Su Wu never left him for so much as a single day. Thinking of him at a distance, Li Ling felt his friend was towering before him, looking even more austere than in the flesh.

Li Ling did not think his own submission to the Xiongnu was a good thing; but he believed that even the most unsympathetic critic would, if he considered all Li Ling had done for his homeland, and what that country had done to him in return, grant that his behavior was "inevitable." But here was a man who, confronted with conditions that were truly "inevitable," absolutely refused to regard them as "inevitable." Hunger, cold, the pain of isolation, the indifference of his homeland, even the near certainty that his painful fidelity would be known to no one—all of these "inevitabilities" taken together were not enough to make him alter his steady attitude of devotion to honor and fidelity.

So Su Wu's existence became to Li Ling both a noble lesson and an irritating nightmare. From time to time he would send people to see if his friend was all right, and to take him foodstuffs, sheep and cattle, and carpets. The desire to see Su Wu and the desire to avoid him were always at war within him.

Several years later, Li Ling once again visited the log cabin by the shores of Lake Baikal. On the way there, he encountered a group of soldiers guarding the area north of Yunzhong and learned from them that recently, in the border regions of Han, everyone from the governor down to the common people was dressed in white. If everyone was wearing white, it could only mean they were in mourning for the emperor. Thus Li Ling learned that Emperor Wu was deceased.

When he arrived at the shores of Lake Baikal and delivered this news, Su Wu faced south and began to wail. He wept and wailed for several days until at last he coughed up blood. Watching this, Li Ling found his own mood gradually darkening. He did not, of course, doubt the sincerity of Su Wu's lamentations. He could not but be moved by such pure and intense grief. But not a single tear came to his own eyes.

True, Su Wu had not suffered the slaughter of his whole family, as had Li Ling. But his elder brother had been involved in a minor road accident during an imperial progress, and his younger brother had failed to capture a criminal as ordered. Each of them had been made to take responsibility for his failings by committing suicide. It would be hard to claim that Su Wu and his family had been well treated by the Han Court. Knowing all this, and seeing with his own eyes Su Wu's sincere and bitter grief, Li Ling suddenly realized that beneath what had earlier appeared to be merely intense stubbornness was an incomparably strong and pure love for the land of Han. It was not something imposed from the outside, like "righteousness" or "fidelity," but the most intimate and natural kind of love, which welled up irrepressibly within Su Wu.

Having come up against this fundamental gap separating him and his friend, he was driven against his will into a dark skepticism regarding himself.

When Li Ling returned south from Su Wu's place of exile, envoys from Han had just arrived. They came to announce the news of Emperor Wu's demise and Emperor Zhao's ascension to the throne, and they also came as a peace mission, seeking to establish friendly relations between the two nations—although such friendly relations had never in the past lasted for as much as a year. There were three envoys, headed, to Li Ling's surprise, by Ren Lizheng, an old friend from his hometown of Longxi.

In the second month of that year, when Emperor Wu died, he was succeeded by the Crown Prince Fu Ling as Emperor Zhao, who was only eight years old. Huo Guang, Master of the Imperial Carriages, was appointed Commander-in-Chief and Generalissimo with responsibility for aiding this child emperor in the work of governance. Huo Guang had been very close to Li Ling in the past, and Shangguan Jie, who had been appointed General of the Left, was also an old friend of Ling's. The two of them had decided to summon Ling back to Han, and that was why former friends of his had been chosen for the current peace mission.

When the official business had been concluded in the presence of the khan, it was time for a festive banquet. Normally it was Wei Lu who acted as host on these occasions, but since the envoys were friends of Li Ling, he was called upon to take part. Ren Lizheng saw Ling, but in front of the assembled high officials of the Xiongnu, he could hardly urge him to return to Han. Seated at a distance from him, he would give Li Ling meaningful looks; from time to time he would stroke the knob at the head of his sword-hilt, trusting that Ling would catch the hidden pun—"knob" and "return" being homophonous in Chinese. Ling did notice, and he understood what Ren was trying to communicate. But he did not know how to respond, what gestures to make.

After the official banquet was over, from the Xiongnu side only Li Ling and Wei Lu stayed on, entertaining the Han envoys with beef and wine and games of chance. It was then that Ren Licheng turned to Ling and said, "A general amnesty has been declared in Han, and everyone is enjoying the benefits of peace and benevolent governance. Since the new emperor is still a child, your old friends Huo Zimeng and Shangguan Shaoshu are helping the sovereign manage the affairs of the empire."

Licheng regarded Wei Lu as having turned into a true Xiongnu, which was in fact the case, so he hesitated to persuade Ling openly in front of the other. He simply brought up the names of Huo Guang and Shangguan Jie, hoping to win Ling over. Ling remained silent, making no reply. After gazing intently at Licheng for a while, he stroked his own hair, which was tied in a queue in Xiongnu fashion, quite unlike that of Han.

When Wei Lu left the room to change clothes, Licheng now for the first time called Ling by his "social name" in an intimate way: "Shaoqing, you have endured many long years of suffering! Huo Zimeng and Shangguan Shaoshu send you their regards." Ling in turn asked how the two high officials were, but in a detached way, and Licheng went on: "Shaoqing, come home! Wealth and rank are not worth talking about. Please make no objections, and come home!" Having just returned from seeing Su Wu, Li Ling was not unmoved by his friend's earnest entreaty. But he knew without having to consider it that it was no longer possible for him to return to Han.

"It would be easy to return. But wouldn't I simply meet with shame again? Is that not so?" Wei Lu returned to the table before Li Ling had finished speaking, and he and Licheng fell silent.

When the party was over and everyone was about to leave, Ren Licheng casually approached Ling and, in a low voice, asked him once more if he truly had no intention of returning to Han. Ling shook his head, and replied that a gentleman could not subject himself to humiliation twice. He said this in a very dispirited way, and it was not because he feared that Wei Lu would overhear him.

Five years later, in the summer of the sixth year of Emperor Zhao's reign, it happened that Su Wu, who had seemed likely to die a wretched death in the far north, unknown to others, was able to return to Han. There is the well-known story of how, attached to the leg of a wild goose brought down by the Han emperor in Shanglin Park was a message from Su Wu written on a strip of silk.

This of course was a fabrication designed to force the hand of the khan, who insisted that Su Wu was dead. A man named Chang Hui, who had come to the nomad territories along with Su Wu nineteen years earlier, met envoys from Han and, informing them that Su Wu was still alive, urged them to save him by means of this subterfuge. Immediately a messenger was sent to Lake Baikal, and Su Wu was escorted back to the khan's court.

Li Ling was truly shaken by this. Whether Su Wu returned to Han or not, his greatness was unchanged; and consequently, there was no change in the mental lashing that Li Ling gave himself. Nonetheless, the notion that Heaven was watching them both struck Ling painfully. It might seem as though Heaven were not watching, but in fact, Heaven was. Li Ling felt fear and awe. Even now he did not think his past actions were by any means wicked; but here was Su Wu, who had boldly accomplished something that made Li Ling ashamed of himself, though in fact he had done nothing unreasonable. Su Wu's accomplishment, moreover, was now made manifest to the world, and that fact told on Li Ling. He feared more than anything else that the unmanly feeling that now wrung his heart might be envy.

Li Ling gave a banquet for his friend prior to parting. There were many things he wished to say. But it all came down to what his resolve had been when he submitted to the Xiongnu. Before he could carry out that resolve, his entire family back home had been slaughtered, and there was no longer any reason to return to Han. But to say that would be to indulge in useless complaining, and he did not say one word about it. But at the banquet's height, unable completely to contain himself, he rose to his feet and began to dance while chanting:

> For ten thousand li I crossed the desert sands,
> As our sovereign's general to fight against the Xiongnu.
> Our way was cut off, our swords and arrows broken,
> Many soldiers perished, and my name too was ruined.
> My aged mother is already dead—
> Though I wish to repay her kindness,
> To what place should I return?

As he sang, his voice trembled, and tears coursed down his cheeks. How unmanly! he rebuked himself, but to no avail.

Su Wu returned to his homeland after nineteen years' absence.

Sima Qian continued writing tirelessly thereafter as well. He had ceased to live in this world and existed only as the characters in his writings. He no longer opened his mouth in real life, but he breathed fire when he borrowed the tongue of the ancient orator Lu Zhonglian. He became Wu Zixu and asked that his eyes be gouged out after his suicide; he became Lin Xiangru and scolded the King of Qin for his impoliteness; he became Prince Dan and, weeping, sent off the would-be assassin Jing Ke. When he described the grief and anger of the worthy but wronged official Qu Yuan of Chu and quoted at length from the famous *Ode on Drowning*, composed as Qu Yuan was about to throw himself into the Miluo River, Sima Qian was almost convinced that the ode was his own creation.

It had been fourteen years since he began his manuscript, and eight years since the calamity of his castration. Around the time that the "Purge of the Sorcerers" and the consequent tragic death of Crown Prince Li took place in the capital, this joint work by father and son had been nearly completed as a comprehensive history, in accordance with the original design. Adding supplementary material and editing and rewriting took several more years. By the time the *Historical Records* in one hundred and thirty fascicles containing five hundred twenty-six thousand, five hundred ideographs was completed, Emperor Wu's life was near its end.

When he laid aside his brush, having finished the autobiographical preface to the seventieth biography, that of the Grand Historian himself, Sima Qian sat in a daze, leaning against his desk. A heavy sigh came from deep within him. His eyes turned for a time toward a stand of scholar trees at the front of his garden, but in truth he saw nothing. His hearing was dulled, yet he seemed to be listening intently to the thrumming of a lone cicada somewhere. He should have been happy, but he was filled instead with a vague, dispirited loneliness and unease.

He felt tense until after he had presented his completed work to the appropriate bureau and formally offered notification to his father before his tomb; but immediately thereafter he was assailed by a terrible lethargy. Like a shaman after the state of possession ends, he was exhausted in body and mind; and although he was just over sixty years old, he seemed to have aged ten years all at once. It appeared that the demise of Emperor Wu and the accession of Emperor Zhao no longer had meaning for the shell of the man who had once been the Grand Historian Sima Qian.

When, as previously related, Ren Licheng and his party visited Li Ling in Xiongnu territory and then returned to the Han capital, Sima Qian was no longer in this world.

We have no accurate records regarding Li Ling after he said farewell to Su Wu, apart from the fact that he died in the Xiongnu lands in the first year of the Yuanping era (74 BCE).

Hulugu Khan, who had been so close to him, had died before him, and had been succeeded by his son, I Iuyandi Khan. But there was civil strife connected with his accession, between Lord Zuoxian and Lord Yululi, and it is not hard to imagine that Li Ling might have been unwillingly drawn into the struggle against the queen mother, Wei Lu, and their confederates.

The *History of the Han* records in its account of the Xiongnu that the son born to Li Ling in the nomad lands supported Commander Wuji as khan and opposed Huhanye Khan, but ultimately failed. This was in Wufeng 2, during the reign of Emperor Xuan—exactly eighteen years after Li Ling's death. We are told only that he was Li Ling's son; his own name is not recorded.

Translated by Paul McCarthy

On Admiration: Notes by the Monk Wujing

After the midday meal, when the Master was resting beneath a pine tree by the roadside, Wukong took Bajie to a grassy patch nearby and made him practice the magic of transformation.

"Try it!" said Wukong. "Think really hard that you want to be a dragon. Think really hard. Wish it with the strongest, most forceful feelings. Abandon all useless thoughts. All right? In earnest. With the greatest intensity."

"All right!" replied Bajie as he closed his eyes and made a Buddhist mudra sign with his hands. The figure of Bajie disappeared, and a green snake, about five feet long, appeared. Looking at this, I could not help bursting out in laughter.

"You fool! Can't you become anything more than a snake?" scolded Wukong. The snake vanished, and Bajie reappeared. "I cannot. I don't know why I cannot," he whimpered shamefacedly.

"You were not concentrating enough. Try it again. Be dead serious—absolutely serious—and keep concentrating on the thought that you want to be a dragon. When you disappear, the only thing remaining is your desire to be a dragon, and then it will happen."

"All right, one more time," said Bajie as he made a mudra sign with his hands. This time, a monstrous creature appeared. It certainly looked like a python, but it also had small forelegs, looking somewhat like a giant lizard. But its belly was fat like Bajie's, and when it crawled a few steps, it was indescribably awkward. I laughed out loud again.

"All right, all right! Stop!" yelled Wukong. Bajie appeared, scratching his head in embarrassment.

Wukong: "It's because your desire to become a dragon isn't strong enough. That's why you cannot do it."

Bajie: "That isn't so. I'm concentrating with all my might, thinking, I want to be a dragon, I want to be a dragon. I'm concentrating as strongly and single-mindedly as I can."

Wukong: "The fact that you cannot do it means that your mind isn't completely focused on the idea."

Bajie: "That isn't fair. You're judging by the results."

Wukong: "True. To criticize the cause only by the results is definitely not the best way to do it. But in this world, it's the surest, most practical way. Your case is a clear example."

According to Wukong, the magic of transformation was as follows: If the desire to become something is strong and pure, then in the end one can become that thing. If one cannot, it means that one's thoughts have not attained that level of strength and purity. Thus, the training for accomplishing the magic of transformation consists of learning to concentrate one's thoughts to make them intense and pure. This training is difficult; however, once that state is achieved, one no longer needs to make the same huge effort. Simply focusing one's mind on the desired form will make it happen. This is the same as with various other arts and practices.

The magic of transformation can be performed by foxes and badgers but not by human beings, because, in the end, human beings have too many things they are concerned with, and it is extremely difficult to achieve spiritual concentration; whereas animals do not have many cares that trouble their mind, it is easy for them to concentrate.

Beyond a doubt, Wukong is a genius. It is something I sensed the moment I first met this monkey. Even though at first I thought he was ugly with his red face and whiskers, the next moment I was overwhelmed by his powerful outpouring of energy and completely forgot about his looks. Now, I even find his appearance beautiful—or at least splendid. His countenance and speech are full of confidence and vitality. He cannot tell a lie—not to others and, above all, to himself. In him a fire is always burning—a great, raging fire. The fire immediately spreads to anyone nearby. Listening to his words, one is compelled to believe as he does. Being near him, one is filled with abundant confidence. In this way he is like the kindling. The world is the wood, ready to be set fire to. Even matters that seem common to us might be, to his eyes, the beginning of a great adventure or a chance for heroism.

He gives meaning to each object or event as he meets it, rather than finding the meaning already in it. The fire within him ignites what is like gunpowder uselessly lying dormant and cold. It is not that he, like an investigator, searches it out; it is rather that, with the heart of a poet, however rough-mannered a poet, he warms everything he comes in contact with (not without the risk of scorching them), causing seeds to sprout and bear fruit. Therefore, to Wukong's eyes, there is nothing ordinary or commonplace. Every morning he rises early, watches the sunrise, and admires its beauty as if seeing it for the first time, sighing in admiration from the bottom of his heart. In awe and amazement, he watches the pine seedling about to emerge from the pine seed.

This is the innocent Wukong, but look at him fight the enemy! What a splendid figure! The heightened intensity of his entire body on alert! Rhythmic yet precise handling of his pole, with no wasted movement! The sense of power when the body tirelessly rejoices, rages, sweats, and jumps! The overflowing of resilience that welcomes any hardship! It is a beauty more fulfilled, naked, vigorous, unselfconscious, and incandescent than the sun in the sky, or a sunflower in bloom, or a cicada at the height of its cry—imagine all this splendor in the fighting figure of that unsightly monkey!

I still recall vividly his clash with the Bull Demon King on Mount Cuiyun a month ago. It so impressed me that I wrote a detailed record of what transpired:

The Bull Demon King has changed his form into a musk-deer and is leisurely eating grass. Wukong senses this fact, turns into a tiger and dashes toward the deer to devour it. The Bull Demon King transforms himself into a large leopard and leaps to meet the tiger, seeking to strike a blow. Wukong becomes a lion, and attacks the leopard. The Bull Demon King changes into a yellow lion, roars like thunder, and tries to tear the lion Wukong apart. Wukong seems to fall to the ground, but in the process becomes a giant elephant. Its trunk is like a python and its tusks resemble enormous bamboo shoots. Unable to counter the elephant, the Bull Demon King reveals his true form, at once becoming a large white bull. Its head is like a mountain peak, its eyes like lightning, and its horns like iron towers. From head to tail it is longer than ten thousand feet; from heel to head it is eight thousand feet. Calling in a loud voice, he says, "You, wicked monkey, whatever are you going to do now?" Wukong reveals his true form, shouts loudly once, and in a twinkling of an eye becomes a hundred thousand feet tall, with his head resembling Mount Tai. His eyes look like the sun and the moon, and his mouth is like a pond of blood in hell. Resolutely he wields his iron pole and strikes at the Bull Demon King, who uses his horns to meet it. The two fight so fiercely that the mountains crumble and the sea boils over, as if heaven and earth were to be turned upside down.

What a magnificent spectacle! It did not occur to me to help Wukong. It was not because I had no worries of defeat for him, the Pilgrim Sun, but because I was embarrassed to add an unskillful brushstroke to a single perfect masterpiece of painting.

Calamity is fuel to Wukong's fire. When he encounters difficulties, it is as if his entire being (both spirit and body) turns to flame. Conversely, when all is calm, he is so dispirited that it is almost comical. Like a top, he will fall unless he is constantly spinning. Even when a difficult situation appears, he envisions a map with a bold line leading directly to his destination. The moment he understands where he is, he sees clearly the path to take. Perhaps it is more accurate to say that he cannot see any other than that path. Like luminous writings in a dark night, only the necessary path floats up; the rest is not to be seen at all. While the slow-witted are stymied, Wukong has already begun the shortest path to his goal. People make much of his bravery and physical strength, taking his extraordinary wisdom little into consideration. But the reason may be that his thought and judgment are so harmoniously blended into his actions.

I know that Wukong is illiterate. I know very well how little learning he has: Even though he was once appointed to the post of Bimawen, an assistant in the Celestial Livery Stable, he neither knew the ideographs of his position nor understood the nature of his work. But this mattered little in the face of his wisdom and physical strength. Sometimes I think that, on the contrary, Wukong must be highly educated. His knowledge concerning fauna, flora, and astronomy is considerable. At a glance, he would be able to gauge an animal's nature, strength, and means of defense. He would know which plants are medicinal and which are poisonous. But if asked to identify these plants and animals by name, he would be found wanting.

Similarly, he could read the stars—discerning direction, time, and season from their position in the heavens—but would not know such names as Virgo or Scorpio. What a difference between him and someone such as myself, who knows the names of all twenty-eight constellations yet cannot find them in the sky! I feel the pathetic dilemma of culture when I face this illiterate monkey!

All parts of Wukong—eyes, ears, mouth, legs, and hands—seem so joyful that they can scarcely contain themselves. They are full of life's energy, and in time of battle, they seem to become so joyous that together they raise a loud shout of happiness, like bees that rush to flowers in summer. Perhaps that is why, despite his seriousness, Wukong seems, when in battle, to be playing.

People speak of "having a resolve to die," but Wukong has no such thing. No matter what kind of danger he finds himself in, he considers only the success or failure of the undertaking (whether it be to subdue monsters or to rescue Master Tripitaka), but not his own life. When he nearly burned to death in the Eight-Diagram Brazier of Laozi, and when he was near to being crushed beneath the mountains Tai, Sumeru, and Omei, in the "Tai Mountain Compression" of the Silver Horn Demon King, he never cried out in fear for his own life.

He experienced great difficulty when the Old Buddha of Yellow Eyebrows trapped him between the gold cymbals at the Little Thunderclap Temple; no matter how much he pushed and poked, the gold cymbals would not break apart. He tried to enlarge his body, but the cymbals stretched, and when he shrank his body, so did the cymbals. When he pulled out his hair, fashioned it into an awl, and tried to bore a hole into the cymbals, he could not even scratch the surface.

In time, Wukong's buttocks grew soft, due to the power of this magical instrument that would melt things. Even then, Wukong was concerned only with the safety of the Master, who had been captured by the monsters; he retained limitless confidence in himself, even as he seemed unaware of it. Eventually, the constellation Gold Dragon came to earth from its celestial realm and pierced the gold cymbals with its iron-like horn. The cymbals reacted as if like human flesh, enveloping the horn, clinging to it and leaving no space through which Wukong could transform himself into a poppy seed and escape. With his buttocks weakening, he finally came upon an idea; he took out his Wish-Granting Hooped Pole, turned it into an awl, bore a hole into the horn of the Gold Dragon, transformed himself into a poppy seed, entered the horn, and had the Gold Dragon pull out its horn.

Freed at last, Wekong forgot all about his softened rump and immediately set to rescuing the Master. Even later, he never mentioned that this had been a close call. It may be that he has never experienced "danger" or worried that "I am finished." It seems he has never even thought about his life or death. When he dies, it will be sudden, perhaps without his realizing it. Until the moment before, he will likely be carrying on energetically as ever. Indeed, one might think his actions grand, but never tragic.

Monkeys are said to mimic others, but this is a monkey that does not copy anyone whatsoever! He never imitates, and he absolutely refuses to accept any idea imposed upon him, even if that idea has been acknowledged for thousands of years. That is to say, he refuses to accept any truth as long as he is not thoroughly convinced of it himself. Neither deep-rooted tradition nor worldly reputation has any authority for him.

Another characteristic of Wukong is that he does not speak of the past. Or, rather, he seems to forget completely what has taken place in the past. About specific events, he has no memory. Rather, the lessons learned from specific events are absorbed into his being and integrated into his spirit and body, thus rendering the events, however bitter, extraneous. I can testify to this, as he never repeats the same tactical error.

But one single terrifying event even Wukong cannot forget. It was the occasion of his first receiving the grace of a meeting with Sakyamuni Buddha, and he recounted to me very seriously the fear he felt at the time.

In those days, Wukong did not know the limits of his own power. When he wore a pair of lotus-thread-woven "Cloud Walking" shoes, slipped into gold mail armor, and wielded the thirteen-thousand-five-hundred-pound gold Wish-Granting Hooped Pole, which he had taken from the Dragon King of the Eastern Sea, no one in the celestial realm or in the earthly realm could match him in battle. He disturbed the Banquet of Celestial Peaches attended by important immortals, and when he was punished by imprisonment inside the Crucible of Eight Diagrams, he broke out and stormed through the celestial realm, venting his fury. He mowed down hoards of heavenly warriors, and he fought for a half day against the Immortal Protector of the Sacred and his thirty-six thunder gods in front of the Palace of Divine Clouds.

As this was going on, Sakyamuni Buddha, the Tathagata, accompanied by the two saints Kasyapa and Ananda, passed by. The Buddha stepped in front of Wukong, blocking his path and halting the fighting. Wukong angrily turned to him. The Buddha asked with a smile, "You seem quite full of yourself, but exactly what of the Way have you mastered?"

Wukong replied, "You do not know the powers that I possess—I who was born from a stone egg on the Flower Fruit Mountain in the state of Aolai, of the Purva-videhah Continent, east of Mount Sumeru. What a foolish fellow you are! I have already mastered the art of maintaining eternal youth. I can ride the clouds, manipulate the winds, and travel eighteen thousand *li* in an instant."

The Tathagata responded, "You should not boast. You will not be able to get off the palm of my hand, let alone fly eighteen thousand *li*."

"What did you say?" retorted Wukong, jumping impulsively onto the palm of the Tathagata's hand. "With my magical powers, I can fly eight hundred thousand *li*. What nonsense to say I will not be able to fly out of the palm of your hand!" Before he finished his sentence, he leapt onto a magic cloud and instantly traveled three hundred thousand *li*. He encountered five large, red pillars, and on the central pillar he inscribed in bold brush strokes these words: "The Great Sage, Equal to Heaven, has visited here." Then he rode the magic cloud again, returned to the Tathagata's palm, and said proudly, "Not only did I fly out of your hand but I flew the great distance of three hundred thousand *li* and left proof of it on a pillar."

"You are a wild, foolish monkey," laughed the Tathagata. "What good are your magical powers? In the last few moments, all you have done is to go back and forth within the palm of my hand. If you do not believe me, look at my middle finger." Wukong looked carefully at the middle finger of Tathagata's right hand, and there, in still fresh brush strokes, written in Wukong's own hand, were the words: "The Great Sage, Equal to Heaven, has visited here."

Startled, Wukong looked up at the Tathagata's face, from which the smile had now disappeared. The Tathagata's eyes were solemn, and staring sternly at Wukong, he expanded to such enormous size as he leaned over Wukong, that he looked as if he would block the heavens. Wukong felt such terror that his blood seemed to freeze, and in panic he tried to jump out of the Tathagata's palm. Immediately, the Tathagata flipped his hand over and, grasping Wukong, transformed his five fingers into the Five-Phases Mountain, confining Wukong under it. On the summit of the mountain, the Tathagata placed a piece of paper with an inscription in gold; it was a mystical Lamaist spell: *Om mani padme hum!* Oh, the *mani* gem atop the lotus flower!

Plunged into dark confusion, as if the world had been turned upside down, Wukong shuddered. In fact, for him the world changed totally. When hungry he ate pellets of iron, when thirsty he drank molten copper. Confined in a cave, he awaited the completion of his term of atonement. He went from extreme arrogance to the loss of all confidence. He grew timid, and in his suffering, he cried loudly, without shame or concern for what others might think. After five hundred years, the monk Tripitaka, who happened to pass by on his journey to India, peeled the mystical spell off the summit of the Five-Phases Mountain and freed Wukong from his imprisonment.

Wukong wept loudly, but on this occasion, it was tears of happiness that he shed. It was simply out of joy and gratitude that Wukong would follow Tripitaka all the way to distant India. It was the purest and strongest form of gratitude.

The terror Wukong experienced by the hand of the Sakyamuni Buddha created an earthly limit in the Wukong of before. It had been an immense existence, in the form of a monkey, predating any distinction between good and evil. But for this immense existence to be of use in earthly life, it was necessary that he be compressed for five hundred years under the weight of the Five-Phases Mountain and to become small. And indeed, how incomparably marvelous, splendid, and large is this smaller Wukong of the present!

Master Tripitaka is a strange person. He is astonishingly weak. Needless to say, he does not know the magic of transformation. If he is attacked by demons and monsters on the road, he is immediately captured. But rather than "weak," it would be more accurate to say that he has absolutely no instinct for self-preservation. Why on earth is it that the three of us are equally attracted to this weak monk Tripitaka?

In truth, it is only I who would think about such matters. Both Wukong and Bajie simply respect and love the Master without knowing why. I think maybe we are drawn to something tragic that is perceived in that weakness of the Master—because it is something that never exists in us, who have risen from the ranks of monsters. The monk Tripitaka has come to understand his own position—and that of human beings, and that of all living beings—in the larger scheme of things, the pity and the preciousness of it.

Moreover, he endures that entire tragedy and then still bravely goes on to seek the good and the beautiful. It certainly is this, the thing that we do not possess and the Master does. True, we have greater physical strength than he. We also know the magical art of transformation. However, once we realize the tragic nature of our existence, we must surely be unable to continue living a righteous and beautiful life. I cannot help but be astonished at this noble strength of our weak Master. Perhaps the Master's charisma comes from his inner nobility hidden within the outward appearance of weakness. According to the interpretation of that impudent Bajie, however, our—or, at least Wukong's—respect and affection for the Master contain a good measure of the homoerotic.

Truly, compared with that genius of action, Wukong, how thick-headed Master Tripitaka is in practical matters! But this is due to the difference in their purpose of living, so it cannot be a matter of discussion. When the Master faces external difficulties, he seeks a way to get through them inwardly, rather than externally. In short, he readies his mind to withstand the shock. No, let me restate that. Without rushing to ready itself, his mind is always positioned, so that his inner self will not be disturbed. He has already prepared his mind so that no matter the misery or the fate, he could still be happy. Therefore, he has no need to seek a solution in the external world. His corporeal defenselessness, which appears so precarious, actually has little effect on his spirit. Wukong would appear to be quite spectacular, but there might be situations in this world that defy solution even by his genius. However, in the Master's case, there is no fear of that. This is because, for the Master, there is no need to solve anything.

For Wukong there is rage, but there is no anguish. There is joy, but there is no melancholy. No wonder he can simply affirm life. What about Master Tripitaka? With that sickly body, the weakness that knows no defense, and the days of constant torment by monsters and demons, still the Master happily affirms life. Is this not extraordinary?

Oddly, Wukong does not understand this quality in which the

Master surpasses him. He thinks that somehow he cannot part from the Master. When he is displeased, Wukong thinks he is following Tripitaka solely because of the golden fillet around his head, which contracts and causes him unbearable pain when he disobeys the monk. And grumbling that "the Master causes so much trouble," he goes to rescue the Master, who has been taken captive by demons. "He is so helpless that I cannot just look on. Why is he like that?" When Wukong speaks this way, he seems to be conceited, feeling better than the weak, but he does not know that in his feelings toward the Master there is a considerable admixture of instinctive awe toward a superior being and yearning for beauty and nobility—feelings that all living beings possess.

What is more amusing is that the Master himself does not know his own superiority over Wukong. Each time he is rescued from the grasp of demons, the Master tearfully thanks Wukong: "If you did not save me, I would have lost my life." But, in actuality, no matter whether he is caught and eaten by demons, the Master will not perish.

It is interesting to look at the two of them, who do not know their true relationship to each other and yet love and respect each other, despite their small disagreements from time to time. However, between these two diametrically opposite characters, there is a single point of commonality. That is, in their way of life, both regard the given as necessity, and feel that necessity is completeness. Furthermore, they regard that necessity as freedom. It is said that diamond and charcoal are composed of the same element. However, it is interesting that the attitude toward life of these two people, who are more different from each other than are diamond and charcoal, derives from this same way of comprehending reality. Moreover, what else can this "equation of necessity and freedom" be, if not a sign of their genius?

Wukong, Bajie, and I are so different from one another that it is comical. Even when the sun sets and no lodging is found and we agree to stay overnight at a dilapidated temple by the roadside, the three of us agree on the basis of different reasoning. Wukong willingly chooses it, thinking that such a dilapidated temple would be the most suitable place for subduing demons. Bajie thinks that it would be too much trouble to seek other lodging at this late hour, when he would like to go indoors and have a meal, and besides he is sleepy. I think, "This area is probably full of evil spirits anyway. If we are going to encounter calamity regardless of where we go, then we might as well do so here." Nothing is more interesting than the ways of living creatures.

Overshadowed by Wukong, the flamboyant Pilgrim Sun, Zhu "The Pig" Wuneng Bajie seems a lesser figure, but he nonetheless possesses unique characteristics. At any rate, this hog is terribly fond of this life, this world. With all of his senses—olfactory, gustatory, tactile—he is attached to and obsessed with this world. Once Bajie told this to me: "What is our purpose in going to India? Is it to accomplish good deeds and be reborn into paradise in the next life? By the way, what kind of place is this paradise? If we are just going to sit on lotus leaves, swaying to and fro, it is useless, is it not? In paradise, will there be the pleasure of sipping and blowing on steaming hot soup, or the pleasure of filling our mouths with aromatic meat with crispy roasted skin? If not, and all they do is live by inhaling the mist, as in the tales of Taoist immortals, then I would hate it! I want no such paradise. Even though there are hardships, this world has wonderful pleasures that make me forget those hardships—so this world is best. At least it is for me."

After saying this, Bajie counted the things that he thought were pleasurable in this world: Slumber in the shade of a tree on a summer day. Bathing in a mountain stream. Playing the flute on a moonlit night. Sleeping late on a spring morning. Pleasant talk by the fireplace on a winter night.... How happily did he name his many pleasures! In particular, when he began to talk about the beauty of the young female body and the flavors of food in each of the four seasons, his words seemed to pour forth. I was astounded. I had never thought that there were so many pleasurable things in this world, and that there was someone tasting those pleasures to the utmost, like him. I realized that, indeed, it takes talent to enjoy them. After that, I stopped holding this pig in contempt.

However, as I began to talk to Bajie more frequently, I came to notice something odd. That is, beneath Bajie's hedonism, a shadow of something uncanny could be glimpsed. Even though he says, "If I did not have respect for the Master and fear of Pilgrim Sun, I would have stopped this difficult journey long ago," a feeling of apprehension and fear, as if he were treading on thin ice, could be detected. That is to say, for that pig—just as for me—there are indications that this journey to India must be the only thread of hope that he could cling to after disillusionment and despair.

In any event, at present, I must learn everything from Pilgrim Sun. There is no time to consider other matters. The wisdom of the Monk Tripitaka and Bajie's way of life should come after I have completed my learning from Pilgrim Sun. I have not yet learned anything from Wukong. Since I left the waters of the River of Flowing Sand, how much progress have I made? Am I not still the same old slow learner as before? Take, for instance, my role in this journey. It is how it is. I stop Wukong from going too far in times of peace, and reprimand Bajie for laziness in daily life. That is all, is it not? I have no active role at all. Would someone like me, regardless of when or where he was born, end up being merely a coordinator, advisor, and observer? Would I be unable ever to become an active doer?

The more I see Pilgrim Sun in action, the more I cannot help thinking this way: "The burning fire probably does not know that it is burning. While we think we are burning, we are not really burning." When I see Wukong's ease, I always think that. "Free action arises naturally from something internal that matures and ripens and in the end compels one to act from within oneself." However, I simply think about it. I have not been able to follow Wukong a single step yet. Although I think often that I have much to learn from him, I am afraid of the immensity of Wukong's aura and the roughness of Wukong's personality, and I cannot get close to him.

In fact, to be honest, any way one looks at it, Wukong is not a very helpful colleague. He has no sympathy for others, and he scolds them mercilessly. He takes his own abilities as the standard and he demands the same from others; when they cannot perform, he berates them. It is intolerable. Perhaps I can say that he is not aware of the extraordinariness of his own abilities. We know he is not mean-spirited. It is simply that he does not understand anyone's lesser abilities, and consequently he has absolutely no sympathy for anyone's doubt, hesitation, or anxiety. He has been known to become so frustrated at people that he explodes in anger.

As long as our lack of abilities does not make him angry, he is really a good-natured, innocent, childlike man. Bajie is constantly being scolded for his oversleeping, laziness, or failure in the magic of transformation. I have not made Wukong angry very much up to now, because I have maintained a distance from him and tried not to expose my weaknesses to him. If I continue to act in this way, I will never be able to learn anything from him. I must get closer to Wukong, and no matter how hard his roughness will be on my nerves, I need to be scolded, struck, and cursed, and then from my side, I should curse back at him, and in that way I must learn from that monkey through my total being. Merely observing and admiring him from a distance will be of no use.

Night. I am awake alone.

Tonight, we could not find lodging, and so the four of us are sleeping on the grass beneath a large tree in a valley. There is only the sound of Wukong's snoring, and its echo against the hills. Each time he snores, dew drops fall down from the leaves above our heads. Although it is summer, the night air is chill, as might be expected. It must already be past midnight.

I have been lying on my back, looking up at the stars peeking through the leaves of the tree. I am lonely. I feel terribly lonely. I feel as if I were standing alone on a lonely star, staring at the night of the pitch-black, cold, empty world. Stars have always made me think of eternity or infinity, so while I cannot avoid looking at the stars, I find it hard to deal with my feelings. Near a large, pale blue star, there is a small crimson star. Far below them, there is a slightly yellow, warm-looking star, and it becomes hidden or visible each time the leaves of the tree sway in the wind.

A shooting star flies by and disappears. It makes me suddenly recall the clear, lonely eyes of the Monk Tripitaka. They are eyes that seem always to be gazing far away, always to be filled with pity. I have not been able to tell in our daily life what this pity is directed toward. But it occurs to me that perhaps now I understand. The Master is always looking at eternity. And he sees clearly the fate of all things on earth. Faced with the extinction that will surely come, wisdom, love, and other such good things still try their best to open their tiny blossoms. Perhaps that is what the Master is constantly watching with eyes full of compassion. While I am looking at the stars, somehow I begin to feel that way. I raise myself and peer at the face of the Master sleeping next to me. While I watch his peaceful face in repose and listen to his quiet breathing, I begin to feel faint warmth in the depths of my heart, as if a small fire has been lit.

(*from* My Journey to the West)
～ *Translated by Nobuko Ochner*

Afterword

This collection of stories about China by the Japanese writer Nakajima Atsushi, or, according to the English convention, Atsushi Nakajima (1909-1942) brings to English-speaking readers a reading experience quite different from that of most contemporary Japanese fiction of the last half-century. There are no cherry blossoms, languishing women, philandering husbands, or mad pursuit of material goods. Instead, the world depicted in Nakajima's works abounds in characters in search not of money, power, or women but of the ultimate meaning of their own lives. It is a precursor to the Existentialist world-view, the fundamental questioning of the meaning of existence, arising from despair over the senseless destruction of war. It is a philosophical stance that became widespread internationally in the decades immediately after World War II. Nakajima predates this philosophical movement by a few years, dying prematurely from asthma in December of 1942. Thus, his proto-Existentialist writings are not influenced by the prevalent trends of his time. Rather, they stem from his abiding personal philosophical preoccupations. He was deeply involved with the question of "the first principles"—why things are what they are, and what the "self" is.

One might ask why Nakajima turned to ancient China for material for his stories, instead of contemporary Japan. What compelled him to write about Confucius and his disciples; about a cavalry commander and a court historian, an archer in quest of the ultimate mastery of his art, dukes' and princes' rise and fall, a poet metamorphosing into a tiger, and a river monster searching for self-identity? Partly it was due to his family and education, partly it was because he lived and wrote in Japan of the late 1930s and early 1940s; and it was also the result of his concept of literature.

Nakajima's grandfather, father, and three of his uncles studied and taught the Chinese classics. He grew up among the texts of ancient Chinese philosophy, history, and literature, gaining familiarity with many of them. This was a time-honored branch of intellectual activity in traditional Japan.

CHINESE CLASSICS IN JAPANESE CULTURE

From the beginning of literate culture in Japan, Chinese influence has been at its core. The writing system of the Chinese language was imported to Japan in the late fourth century, as part of the introduction of the advanced civilization of China. At that time the Japanese language did not yet have its own writing system. The situation was analogous to Latin, or Roman, letters serving as the basis of the alphabet later used in most of the European languages. The writings of the Nara Period (eighth century), the first important historical period in Japan, used a unique system of appropriating Chinese characters to represent Japanese sounds, in addition to using Chinese sentences while construing them as Japanese. In the ninth century, the Japanese kana syllabaries were developed, enabling Japanese writers to record their words directly, without translating into Chinese or finding appropriate Chinese characters for Japanese sounds.

Despite the invention of a syllabic writing system, the Japanese people, through the millennia, continued to read, learn from, and adapt the Chinese classics, just as Nakajima did. The Confucian texts of the

"Four Books and Five Classics," such as *The Analects, Mencius, Great Learning,* and *The Classic of Poetry,* became the canon for educated Japanese men. Additionally, other classical texts were regularly studied, such as *The Historical Records (Shiji)* by the Grand Historian of China, Sima Qian (145-86 BCE), which is the prototype of official Chinese historiography; *The Spring and Autumn Annals,* particularly the version with Commentaries by Master Zuo; the Daoist writings of Laozi and Zhuangzi, to name but a few. Anecdotes and quotations from such classics were immediately recognizable to educated men of East Asia, much as the knowledge of Greek and Roman myths, Biblical anecdotes and quotations, Arthurian legends, Chaucer and Shakespeare became the mark of educated men and women in Western culture. Nakajima's stories make use of almost all the above-mentioned classics in varying degrees.

Chinese poetry had an enormous influence on the development of poetry in Japan, including the early anthologies of poetry in Chinese composed by Japanese poets, which were compiled by order of the imperial court. A side-by-side compilation of Chinese and Japanese poetry was popular among the aristocrats of the early Heian Period (794-1185). Such Chinese poets as Li Bo (or Li Bai), Du Fu, and Bo Juyi, were known to every educated person. In *The Tale of Genji,* for instance, Murasaki Shikibu refers to the celebrated beauty Yang Gueifei from Bo Juyi's "Song of Everlasting Sorrow." Many motifs from Chinese poetry, including Yang Gueifei as femme fatale, recur in Japanese literature throughout its history, enabling intertextual reading.

The importance of poetry in traditional East Asian culture is illustrated in Nakajima's story "The Moon over the Mountain" (Sangetsu-ki, 1942), a story of a Chinese intellectual who aspires to become a great poet but turns into a tiger. The man first wants to obtain high rank as a bureaucrat; but failing that, he devotes his life to poetry composition, only to find that this ambition too will not be realized. That a bureaucrat wishes to excel in poetry has a particular resonance in the ancient Chinese setting. Since the official civil service examination system tested one's knowledge of the classics and history, and one's ability to compose poetry, these types of writing had great prestige and value.

In the Chinese tradition, historical writings, including biographies and poetry, were privileged over narrative fiction because of Confucian disapproval of fictional tales as "small talk" (*xiaoshuo*), i.e., insignificant and lacking in truth value. In contrast to poetry, fiction writing was an avocation in traditional China, often performed under pseudonyms. Some of the early examples of Chinese narrative fiction, which influenced Japanese readers and writers, drew heavily on history and folklore. Such examples include *The Romance of the Three Kingdoms* and *Water Margin*. These early works set a model for tales of heroic deeds or of loyalty for Japanese readers throughout the ages, starting with translations into Japanese, adaptations of characters and episodes, and even free re-interpretations. During the Edo Period (1600-1868), for example, two writers mainly wrote on Chinese topics: Ueda Akinari (1734-1809) and Takizawa Bakin (1767-1848). Ueda Akinari's *Tales of Moonlight and Rain* include an adaptation of the Chinese tale of a white snake with magical powers and create a new tale of possession and bewitchment. Bakin read extensively in Chinese and Japanese classics, such as *Water Margin*, to create his didactic tales of loyalty and honor, as in *Satomi and the Eight "Dogs."* A more fantastic Chinese narrative fiction is *The Journey to the West*, a fictionalized telling of the historical journey of the Tang monk Xuan Zang to India to bring the Buddhist scriptures to China. *The Journey to the West* served as the main source of Nakajima's fantastic intertextual stories about the river monster Wujing, with the blending of a significant amount of Western philosophy.

Chinese learning was still the foundation of education in the early Meiji Era, until the First Sino-Japanese War (1894-1895). Such writers as Mori Ôgai (1862-1922) and Natsume Sôseki (1867-1916) were educated first in classical Chinese, before they learned Western languages: Dutch and German for Ôgai, English for Sôseki. Both writers excelled in these Western languages to such a degree that they were selected by the government to study in Europe. Nonetheless, Ôgai kept his diary in Chinese while he stayed in Berlin (1884-1888), and his novel titled *The Wild Goose* (1911-1913) refers to the classical Chinese novel *Plum in the Golden Vase*. Mori Ôgai's writings were the subject of Nakajima's study during his brief stint at the Tokyo Imperial University graduate school (1933-1934). Natsume Sôseki wrote poetry in Chinese for diversion when his fiction writing depressed him, particularly in writing his last uncompleted novel *Light and Darkness* (1916). During the Taishô Era (1912-1926), a number of novelists wrote stories and plays about Chinese historical or literary figures, such as Li Bo and Su Dongpo, by Satô Haruo (1892-1964) and Tanizaki Jun'ichirô (1886-1965) respectively. Folk or religious tales of China also appealed to such writers as Akutagawa Ryûnosuke (1892-1927), who made use of some tales set in ancient China, such as the Buddhist miracle tale "Toshishun" (Chinese: Du Zichun).

In the early years of the subsequent Shôwa Era (1926-1989), however, this trend changes drastically. During the late 1930s and early 1940s, when Nakajima wrote stories about China, he was in the minority of writers choosing this time-honored subject matter. This change in attitude was probably due to a series of conflicts that Japan engaged in on the Chinese continent, including the Manchurian Incident of 1931, the establishment of the puppet-state of Manchuguo in 1932, and the China Incident of 1937, also known as the Second Sino-Japanese War, which led into the Pacific War of 1941-45.

In the postwar era and beyond, Japanese writers generally showed more interest in modern China. However, some writers still took an interest in ancient China. For example, Takeda Taijun (1912-1976) wrote about Sima Qian, the Grand Historian of China. Takeda seems to use this vehicle to discuss his view of history, historical records, and society. Inoue Yasushi (1907-1991) is another postwar writer who wrote on Chinese topics in his historical novels. These include *Journey beyond Samarkand*, *The Roof Tile of Tempyô*, *Dunhuang*, *Loulan*, and *Confucius*. In the novel *Confucius*, Inoue portrays the sage as a teacher for mankind, who preached a practical way of bringing order to a chaotic age, by applying the family model to the government: ruler as benevolent and wise father and subjects as obedient and loyal children. Confucius was respected but not accepted by the rulers of various states throughout his wanderings. Inoue at times expanded on the historical records according to his novelistic needs.

NAKAJIMA'S CHOICE OF CHINESE MATERIAL

Nakajima Atsushi's manner of using Chinese sources, in contrast to that of Inoue Yasushi, for example, is mostly faithful to the classical source texts, keeping changes to a minimum. Nakajima's treatment of Confucius and his disciples in "The Disciple" (1943), for example, weaves several sources together to create a dynamic story of human interaction, yet he does not easily take liberties with the situations, ideas, or characterizations. The development of the disciple Zilu from an impetuous young man who disdained learning to a Confucian gentleman who insists on dying as a proper gentleman in accordance with his moral code illustrates both the extent of Confucius' influence and the limits of education to alter one's nature. It shows that even the great teacher Confucius could not change the core values of Zilu, who placed loyalty above intelligent self-preservation. In telling the story of the famous teacher and his most devoted student, Nakajima brings out the account already embedded in the Confucian texts and other related writings. It is important to note that this "respect for the classical sources" is a characteristic that distinguishes Nakajima as a writer from Akutagawa, although some critics have compared Nakajima to Akutagawa on the basis of the two writers' predilection for using classical source texts. Akutagawa generally reinterprets the events and characters from a modern skeptical perspective, probing the hidden motives and darker emotions of human beings. By contrast, Nakajima focuses on larger, more fundamental issues of human existence—how one should find oneself, how one should live in an unjust world.

THE CONTEXT OF NAKAJIMA'S WORKS

In Japanese literature of the modern period, the trend has been to move away from Chinese influence toward Western influence. In

Nakajima's day, however, the specific circumstances of Japanese history were conducive to his drawing on these classics that were second nature to him, having grown up in a family steeped in Chinese studies. Because of the increasing censorship within Japan in the 1930s and early 1940s, writers were forced to produce works supporting the Japanese government's policy, or to write something totally unrelated to the time. Nakajima's personal essay written in 1942 expresses his view that literature should be separate from politics, and that if one did not have a topic one truly wished to write about, one should not write. Writing about ancient China was a way of expressing his own existential search for the meaning of self and of the world in a society that severely limited what one could write. In the novella *Li Ling*, Nakajima contemplated the severe fate that befell the historical Sima Qian, the general Li Ling whom Sima Qian defended, and another man, Su Wu, who was detained by the enemy for nineteen years: the unfairness and injustice of it all, along with the ineffectual yet necessary struggles of the individual, seemed to parallel the circumstances that faced many Japanese people of his day.

NAKAJIMA ON LITERATURE

Nakajima had another reason for choosing to write about someone else, outside Japan and in the remote historical past, rather than about himself. He had found through his earlier efforts to write about his own philosophical preoccupations in an autobiographical fashion that such works are limited and limiting as literature. It was true that much of modern Japanese fiction by "serious" writers tended to be autobiographical, for two main reasons: one was the influence of Naturalism, which was imported from the West in the early twentieth century and underwent a peculiarly Japanese transformation, in which unadorned descriptions and frank confessions of one's personal life were valued for their truthfulness or authenticity; the other reason was the continuing importance of the traditional Japanese aesthetic value of *makoto* (sincerity, or truthfulness). However, despite such privileging of autobiographical fiction in the Japanese literary establishment, Nakajima came to realize that his life as a schoolteacher was not interesting enough material or a broad enough canvas to depict the general human condition: the search for meaning in a possibly meaningless world. He chose instead to tell the story of his philosophical wanderings by describing the struggles of the protagonist, a completely fictitious character, in "The Rebirth of Wujing."

NAKAJIMA IN JAPANESE LITERARY HISTORY

Generally speaking, writers in Japan who produced excellent works on classical Chinese topics receive great respect, if not a great popular following. The case of Bakin in the Edo Period was mentioned above. He was highly respected by those readers who could read his books, not only in his day but throughout the nineteenth century. In the case of Nakajima, he was a virtually unknown writer until shortly before he died from asthma at age thirty-three in December of 1942. He had just made his literary debut with the publication of two stories in February of 1942, then published a long work in May, and two collections of stories in the summer of 1942, becoming a candidate for the Akutagawa Prize in September, just before his sudden death. Within a short time after his death, however, his complete works were published, in 1948. Since then, four subsequent editions of his complete works have been published as of 2009, a hundred years after his birth. His stories, particularly "The Moon over the Mountain," have become well established in the Japanese canon by being incorporated into high school textbooks. Although the original Japanese texts written in Nakajima's classical, erudite style are not easy, significant numbers of readers are strongly devoted to Nakajima's writings. The young Kyôgen performer Nomura Mansai, for instance, is one of the devoted readers of Nakajima's stories, and Nomura has recently produced a number of dramatic stage performances of Nakajima's stories, using the techniques of the classical Kyôgen, a performance genre that emerged in the medieval period as comic interludes performed between serious No dramas.

NAKAJIMA IN THE WORLD

Atsushi Nakajima has a secure place in Japanese literary history, and Japanese readers will likely be attracted to Nakajima's stories in the future as well. On the world scene, Nakajima's writings as translated into Western languages are more readily accessible to general readers, without the immediate and palpable challenge of his classical learned style with its difficult Chinese ideographs. The contents of his stories remain vital and relevant, regardless of geographical differences or the passage of time, because they are concerned with the fundamental questions of being human—not just from a Japanese or Chinese perspective, but from a philosophical standpoint that encompasses both East and West. Intertextuality, including the blending of East and West, is one of the key elements in Nakajima's texts, giving them richness, resonance, depth, and longevity.

Nobuko Ochner and Paul McCarthy